THE
FARTHEST-AWAY
MOUNTAIN

DELL YEARLING BOOKS are designed especially to entertain and enlighten young people. Patricia Reilly Giff, consultant to this series, received her bachelor's degree from Marymount College and a master's degree in history from St. John's University. She holds a Professional Diploma in Reading and a Doctorate of Humane Letters from Hofstra University. She was a teacher and reading consultant for many years, and is the author of numerous books for young readers.

THE FARTHEST-AWAY MOUNTAIN

LYNNE REID BANKS

ILLUSTRATED BY VICTOR AMBRUS

A Dell Yearling Book

Published by
Dell Yearling
an imprint of
Random House Children's Books
a division of Random House, Inc.
New York

Originally published in Great Britain by Abelard-Schuman Limited in 1976. First American edition published by Doubleday Books for Young Readers in 1977.

Visit us on the Web! www.randomhouse.com/kids

Educators and librarians, for a variety of teaching tools, visit us at www.randomhouse.com/teachers

ISBN: 0-440-41926-3

Reprinted by arrangement with Delacorte Press

Printed in the United States of America

January 2004

10 9 8 7 6 5 4 3 2 1

OPM

CONTENTS

A PREFACE

ONCE UPON A TIME, in a little village that lay in a mountain valley, there lived with her family a girl called Dakin.

Her country was beautiful. The air there was so clear that it sparkled in the sunshine as if it were made of diamond dust. Every morning, winter or summer, Dakin could look out of her bedroom window and see the farthest-away mountain, its black peak standing up clear of the thick shawl of pinewoods it wore on its lower slopes. Between the peak and the woods was a narrower shawl of snow. This snow changed color in a most odd way. Sometimes it was a sharp blue, and sometimes purple, or pink, or even yellow, or green. Dakin would watch this snow in great puzzlement, for snow, after all, is supposed to be white.

She looked at the pinewoods, too. Forests always gave Dakin a shivery feeling, half unease and half excitement. There was no knowing what lay beneath those close-together branches, and no one could tell her, because no one in the town—not even her father, who had visited the city and the ocean—had ever been to the farthest-away mountain.

Old Deegle, the ballad singer and storyteller who came once a year to bring them news and tales from all over the country, said that the reason no one had ever been to the farthest-away mountain was that however long you traveled toward it, it always stayed in the distance. This, he said, was due to a spell that had been placed on it by a magician from their very own village whose wicked son had disappeared into the mountain long, long ago.

But now that you know as much as anyone then knew about the farthest-away mountain, I must tell you about Dakin. She is the most important person in the story.

Dakin was small and dainty and wore full skirts to her ankles over lots of petticoats, but no shoes except when it was very cold, and then she wore lace-up boots. She had long hair, so fair as to be almost white. She was supposed to keep it in plaits, but usually she didn't, and it blew out behind her and got tangled; then her mother would have to brush and comb it for hours to get all the knots out. She had a turned-up nose and eyes the color of the blue mountain flowers that grew in spring, and small brown hands and feet. She was fourteen.

In those days a girl was quite old enough to get married by that age. Dakin was the prettiest girl in the village; she could sing like a thrush and dance like a leaf in the wind, and besides, she was a marvelous cook. So that, until you know certain other things about her, it's difficult to understand why her parents were so very anxious about her chances of getting married.

It had begun four years earlier, when she was ten and had announced to her mother and father and two sisters and two brothers that she was not going to marry until she had seen some of the things she wanted to see, and done some of the things she wanted to do. She went on to tell them that there were three main things, which were these: She wanted to visit the farthest-away mountain; she wanted to meet a gargoyle; and she wanted to find a prince for her husband.

The family was at supper at the time. Her father and mother had looked at each other, and so had her brothers and sisters. Then they all looked at Dakin, who was calmly drinking her soup.

"But Dakin, you can't go to the farthest-away mountain," said her father. "No one's ever been there, not even me, and I'm the most traveled man in the village."

"Dakin, what do you want to see a gargoyle for?" cried her mother. "If you ever saw one, you'd be so frightened you'd turn into stone."

"You're a silly goose," said her elder brother, Dawsy.

Dakin had stopped drinking her soup and was looking

out of the window toward the farthest-away mountain, which in the clear air looked as if it were just beyond the end of the village. "I must go to the farthest-away mountain and see what's in the forest," she said. "And I want to find out what makes the snow change color."

"There's nothing in the forest that you won't find in our own pinewood," argued Margle, her second brother, who thought he knew everything. "And I can tell you why the snow changes color, without you going to see: It's the sun shining on it."

"Shining *blue*? Shining *green*?" said Dakin scornfully.

"The gargoyle part's silly, though," said her littlest sister, Triska, who was only six. "I've seen pictures of them in Pastor's book of church pictures, and they're horried and ugly."

"I think they look sad," said Dakin. "I want to find one and ask why gargoyles look sad."

"They're only statues of heads. They can't *talk*!" scoffed Sheggie with her mouth full. "Anyway," she added with some satisfaction, "you'll have to give in about the prince. There's only Prince Rally, and he can't marry anyone until the Ring of Kings is found."

"Which might be any time," said Dakin.

"Which will be never," said Margle. "It's been missing for seventeen years, since it was stolen by a troll at Prince Rally's christening. And no one in the royal family can get married without it."

"Besides," said Sheggie, "what makes you think he'd

marry you? He'd want to marry a princess." But a dreamy look came into her eyes, so that Dawsy, who was a tease, said, "Look at Sheggie, wishing he'd come and ask *her*!" And they all laughed.

Dakin's brothers and sisters forgot what she'd said, and her father and mother hoped Dakin had forgotten too. Four years went by, and young men began to ask for her hand in marriage. But when her father would tell her that this one or that one had asked for her, Dakin would only shake her head.

"It's no good, Father," she would say. "I've made up my mind to visit the farthest-away mountain, and see a gargoyle, and find a prince to be my husband."

Her father at first tried to reason with her, and later he got angry and shouted, and as time went by he grew pathetic and pleaded, which was hardest of all for Dakin, who loved him, to resist. But her mind was made up and somehow she couldn't change it.

So now she was nearly fifteen and there was hardly a young man in the village who had not asked for her at least once and gone away disappointed. Sheggie and Dawsy and Margle were all married, so that left only Triska at home to keep her company. But she seemed quite happy, and usually sang as she did her work around the house; only sometimes, on her way past a window or across the grass outside the back door, she would stop with a dishcloth or a plate of chicken meal in her hands and look to the left, along the valley to where the royal estates lay, with the spires, high walls, and shining golden gates of the palace.

Then she would turn and look the other way, toward the mountain. She would stand quite still, as if listening; then she would sigh very deeply before moving on again.

1
THE CALL

ONE MORNING, VERY EARLY, Dakin woke up sharply to find herself sitting up in bed.

"Somebody called me!" she thought. "I heard a voice in my sleep!"

She jumped up and ran to the open window in her long nightgown. Outside, the sun was just appearing beyond the farthest-away mountain, breathing orange fire onto the strange, patchwork snow and streaking the pale sky with morning cloud colors. It was still cold, and Dakin shivered as she called softly into the empty world:

"Did somebody want me?"

No one answered, and Dakin thought she must have

dreamed it. But just as she was turning to jump back into bed again, she saw something that nearly made her fall out of the window.

The mountain nodded.

At least, that's what it looked like. As the sun almost burst over the top, the black head of the mountain seemed to dip, as if to say, "Yes, somebody wants you."

Dakin stared and stared, forgetting the cold, until the sun was completely clear of the peak and stood out by itself, round and red and dazzling. Nothing else happened, but all the same, Dakin knew. It was time to start.

Moving quickly and quietly, she put on her warmest dress with three red petticoats under it, her stout climbing boots that laced with colored lacings up past her ankles, and the white apron she always wore. She hadn't time to plait her hair, so she pushed it out of the way under her long white stocking cap. Then she tiptoed downstairs.

It was difficult to be quiet because of the boots, which she should have left till later. Her mother called from her bedroom:

"Dakin, is that you?"

"Yes, Mother," said Dakin, wondering how she would explain her going-out clothes if her mother saw her.

"Put on the water for the porridge, little one," called her mother sleepily.

Dakin almost changed her mind about going that moment. She wanted to run into her parents' room and curl up under the big feather quilt, hugging her mother's feet as she used to when she was little. It would be so safe and happy to put the water on the big black stove for the porridge, and later to eat it with coffee and wheaty bread with Mother and Father and Triska, and feed the hens and do the washing and go on all day as if the farthest-away mountain had never called her.

For a moment she paused on the stairs. Then she thought, "No. I must do what I've said I'll do."

So she went on downstairs, and pumped the water very quickly, and put it on to heat. Then she hastily filled her knapsack with the things she thought she'd need—a chunk of bread and another of cheese, a slab of her mother's toffee, a mug and a knife, a candle and some matches. Then she looked around. On the window ledge was a book of poems her father had brought back for her from the city, and she put that in.

Then, as an afterthought, she lifted off the mantelpiece the little brass figure of a troll that her father had found years and years ago on the very edge of the pinewood. She held the little man in her hand and looked at his impish, bearded face under the pointed hat.

"I shouldn't take you really," she whispered. "You're brass and you're heavy."

But nonetheless she slipped him into her knapsack and felt him slide between the loaf and the book and lie at the bottom. And she didn't feel so lonely suddenly.

Now she could definitely hear sounds of movement from above, and she knew that soon they'd be down. So she

pulled her warm brown cloak down from the hook behind the back door and wrapped it around her; then she put all her weight on the heavy latch, and the next moment she was out in the bright morning, running, running toward the farthest-away mountain with her white stocking cap flying out behind her and her knapsack bumping.

First she had to go through the village, or rather across a corner of it. People she knew were just opening up their shutters and putting their bolsters and sheets on the up-stairs window ledges to air.

"Good morning, Dakin!" they cried as she passed. "Where are you off to in such a hurry?"

"I'm going to the farthest-away mountain," she called back over her shoulder. But they all thought she was joking, and laughed, and let her go.

2
THE WICKED WOOD

SOON SHE HAD LEFT the village behind. She climbed a little green hill and ran down the other side, and when she looked back she couldn't see any of the village except the tip of the church steeple. She crossed a rushing, mint-green river by jumping from rock to rock, and then she was as far away from home as she'd ever been. The children of the town were never allowed to go beyond the river alone, because beyond the river was the wood, and the wood could be dangerous, even in daytime. Under the thick pine branches it was always like dusk, and every direction looked the same, so that it wasn't just easy to get lost, it was almost impossible not to.

Dakin paused on the dark edge of the wood and looked

back over the sunny-smooth meadows with their knuckles of rock and the gay foaming river dashing on its way to the sea. She looked ahead, but being under the first branches she couldn't see the farthest-away mountain anymore, only the murky depths of the forest, its tree trunks filling in the spaces between each other until there seemed to be a solid wall of them.

"How will I know that I'm going straight toward the farthest-away mountain, and not walking in circles like Meggers Hawmak when he went in after his cow and was lost for three days?" she wondered.

"Better go back," whispered a little voice inside her head, "before it's too late."

Dakin took a step back toward the rushing river, and then stopped.

"No," she said aloud, and started off under the trees.

Before she'd been walking for three minutes everything around her grew dim and every direction looked the same. She turned to look back the way she had come, but it was just as closed in behind as ahead, with only little trickles of sunshine penetrating the thick pine needles. When she turned to go on she found she didn't know whether she'd turned in a half circle or a whole circle, whether she was going back toward the village or on toward the mountain or in another direction altogether. There were no friendly sounds of birds or scurryings of little animals, no sounds when she walked on the spongy needles and moss, no hum of insects or whisper of breeze—in fact, no sounds anywhere at all.

"I'm frightened!" realized Dakin. It was for the first time in all her life and it was a horrible feeling.

She had never felt so completely alone. She felt tears pricking her eyes like pine needles. And then she remembered.

She wasn't *quite* alone, after all. She had the little troll.

Quickly she slipped undone the straps of her knapsack, opened it, and reached to the bottom between the rough loaf and the smooth book. Her fingers touched the small, heavy figure and closed around it. It fit her hand in a comforting way. She drew the little man out and looked at him. He reminded her of home and the warm kitchen. A tear fell off her cheek and splashed on his long brass goblin's nose.

He sneezed.

Dakin shrieked and dropped him in the moss. She backed against a tree, her eyes huge and her hands to her face.

The little troll picked himself up. He stood knee-deep in moss with his hands on his hips, looking up at her. For a long moment they stared at each other. Then the little man, in a voice like the faraway cracking of twigs, said:

"Could I borrow your handkerchief, madam?"

Without speaking, Dakin took it out of the pocket of her apron and gingerly held it out to him as if expecting him to bite her. He reached up his tiny hand, and holding the handkerchief by one corner with most of it on the ground, he wiped her tear off his face and carefully dried his beard.

"Thank you," he said politely. "I'm quite tarnished enough," he added. "Moisture doesn't do brass any good, you know." He sounded a little bit severe about it.

Dakin went down on her knees beside him, staring at him, quite unable to believe it.

"Would you mind explaining," she said shakily, "how you come to be alive?"

"Certainly," replied the little figure. "Only would you please pick me up? I'm getting a bit tired of shouting."

Cautiously she laid her hand palm-upward on the moss beside him and he stepped briskly onto it, holding on to her thumb to steady himself as she got carefully to her feet. She looked at him in bewilderment. Of course, it was darkish and difficult to be sure, but he seemed just the same—that is, he hadn't turned into a flesh-and-blood little man. He was still heavy for his size, and he still seemed to be made of brass. Only now he was definitely and undoubtedly alive. He was rubbing at his sleeves to try to get the tarnish off them, and gradually the metal was becoming brighter.

"That's better!" said the troll.

"We did our best," said Dakin, "but we couldn't get into the cracks."

"Quite. Quite," said the troll. "I'll soon have it all off. Now we must talk. By the way, where are you going?"

"To the farthest-away mountain," said Dakin.

The little man was so startled he had to grab her thumb with both hands to save himself toppling to the ground.

"You don't mean—not to the—f-f-f-farthest-away mountain?" he whispered in a trembling voice.

"Why not?" asked Dakin.

"But you can't! No one's ever been there! It's inhabited by gargoyles—"

"Gargoyles?" cried Dakin excitedly.

"Yes. And ogres and monsters and witches and—"

"If no one's ever been there, how do you know?" asked Dakin.

The troll clapped his hand to his mouth, as if he had said too much.

"Well, I—I don't really *know*—that is, I've *heard*—" he stammered.

"You've *been* there! You *have*!" cried Dakin.

"Well—"

"*Haven't* you?"

"Well, as a matter of fact . . . I have. In fact I used to live there. Once. Years and years and years ago. And I don't want to go back!" he added. "So you'd better go straight home like a sensible girl, and put me back on the mantelpiece where it's safe."

"I've *got* to go to the farthest-away mountain," said Dakin. "It called to me."

"What!" The little troll sat down suddenly in the palm of her hand. He looked up and clasped his knotty little hands together as if pleading with her. "It didn't—by any chance—nod to you, too, did it?"

"Yes, it did . . . this morning," said Dakin.

"Then you're done for. Poor little girl. Done for," whispered the troll, shaking his head sadly. A brass tear rolled down the side of his nose. Then he stood up again sharply.

"Well," he said, straightening his pointed hat, "I must be getting along." He walked briskly to the edge of her hand and would have stepped off into empty air if she hadn't grabbed him.

"Wait!" she cried, holding him while he struggled and kicked. "Stop! You can't leave me here alone! Where are you going?"

"Anywhere!" he said. "Anywhere but where you're going. Let me go this minute!"

"But you'll get lost in the wood!" Dakin said. "I don't know myself which direction leads toward home. And you were in the knapsack, so you can't know either."

The troll stopped struggling and looked at her.

"I can find the way out of the wood," he said. "Or I could find the way up the farthest-away mountain. If I wanted to. Which I don't. If the mountain's called you, and nodded to you, well, you have to go. I understand that. So I'll show you which way to walk, and I'll walk in the opposite direction. I wouldn't go there again, not for a million golden pinecones."

With a sinking heart, Dakin put the little man gently down onto the ground and picked up her knapsack.

"All right, then," she said. "I'll go on alone. Which way is it?"

The little man pointed. "That way," he said. "And if you want to keep straight, watch how the pine needles lie. Walk along them, never across. Oh—" He stopped, and dug in a hidden pocket of his jacket. "You'd better take this. You'll never get past Drackamag without it." He held something up to her. When she took it, it turned out to be what looked like a tiny blue bead.

"What is it?" she asked.

"It's to suck," the troll explained. "When you hear Drackamag roaring up ahead, put it in your mouth. Suck. Don't chew." He started to turn away, but again stopped. "One more thing," he said. "Mark you, I wouldn't give a bee sting for your chances of getting through alive, but there's no reason to go without knowing *anything*. You must bathe in the Lithy Pool. That's very important. With all your clothes on." He paused. "I don't know the password anymore," he said sadly. "It used to be 'dragon's fin,' but it might be almost anything now. Perhaps someone will tell you on the way. There used to be Old Croak . . . but he's probably dead long ago. Oh dear." Another brass tear sparkled among the mosses. "Good-by." He turned away very quickly and ran off as fast as his short legs would carry him.

3
THE CABIN IN THE MEADOW

IF DAKIN HAD FELT lonely and frightened before, she felt five times as bad now that her only friend had deserted her. But he had given her *some* help, and she supposed she couldn't blame him for not wanting to come if it was as bad as he said.

She trudged on through the silent trees, her eyes on the ground to watch the way the pine needles lay. They pointed her direction like arrowheads. The absolute quiet was like a heavy blanket over her head. She tried to sing, but her voice just came out in a little bleat.

And all the time, her heart was full of fears.

What—or who—was Drackamag? If he—or it—was as terrible as he sounded, what good was sucking the little blue sweet going to do against him? What was the Lithy Pool, and why should she have to bathe in it with all her clothes on? Who would ask her for the password, and what would happen to her when she didn't know it? And who was Old Croak? He sounded as if he might be helpful if he were still alive. It would be good to feel she had at least one friend ahead of her.

While she was thinking about all this, and following the pine needles, she suddenly noticed that there were little dapples of light on them. She looked up and to her delight discovered that the trees were thinning.

She had reached the other side of the wood!

Through the last of the rough trunks, she could see a sunny meadow, speckled with flowers. In the middle of it was a little log cabin, and beyond that the farthest-away mountain stood up against the sky, looking not far away anymore but very near. She laughed aloud and began to run.

Just as she passed the last tree, she felt a sudden tug, and the next moment her hair came tumbling down her back. She stopped and looked back. Her bobbled stocking cap was caught on a branch, high, high up.

She stood under the last tree, staring above her at the cap.

"But how could it have got up there?" she thought. "I can't possibly reach it!" It was as if one of the high branches had reached down and snatched the cap off her head as she passed. She thought of climbing up to get it, but the tree was smooth all the way up.

"I'll just have to leave it," she thought. "Oh *dear*!"

But nothing seemed so bad now she was out in the sunny meadow and away from the gloom of the wood. The birds sang as she ran through the deep grasses to the cabin, with the heads of the long-stemmed buttercups bouncing off her skirts. The place seemed deserted. She peered in at one of the windows, but the glass seemed to be covered with dust inside so that she couldn't see. She went around to find the door. She turned one corner, and another, and another, and—but here was the same window again! There was no door.

"But how do people get in and out?" she wondered aloud.

"They don't," said a voice that sounded like an old rusty pump. "That's the idea."

Dakin jumped. The voice had seemed to come from inside the house.

"Where are you?" she asked, looking through the window again.

The dust on the inside of the pane was disturbed, and now Dakin could see something—it looked like a little hand—rubbing a tiny clear place. Then the hand disappeared, and there was a minute eye, looking out at her.

There was a pause while the eye looked her up and down. Then the voice said: "You look all right. You can come in if you want to."

Dakin wasn't at all sure she did, but it seemed rude not to, so she said:

"How can I, as there's no door?"

"Down the chimney, of course," said the voice impatiently.

Dakin looked around. Leaning against the side of the cabin was a ladder, which she hadn't noticed before, and up this she climbed rather reluctantly. She thought how dirty the chimney was at home and wished she'd gone straight past the cabin without stopping.

"Come on, come on!" the voice called irritably.

On the roof, Dakin scrambled to the chimney stack and looked down. It was a very big opening, and it didn't look sooty, so she sat on the edge of it with her legs dangling in.

"Don't be afraid; you won't hurt yourself!" called the voice.

Dakin was getting very curious to see what the owner of the voice looked like, so she pushed herself off the rim of the chimney.

It was rather like going down a slide: There was a quick whoosh, and the next thing she knew was that she was standing in a big, open fireplace that obviously hadn't had a fire in it for years, if ever. She looked around. The inside of the cabin was just one room, very small and bare; it had plants growing in pots here and there, and that was about all in the way of furniture, but the most curious thing was a pool, sunk into the floor, with lily pads floating on it; and up above it a big silvery green witch ball dangled like a moon.

Dakin looked for the owner of the voice, but couldn't see anyone.

"Hello," croaked the rusty voice. "Here I am."

Dakin stared. Sitting on one of the lily pads on the pond was the biggest, oldest, wartiest frog she had ever seen. It came to her in a flash who it must be.

"You're Old Croak!" she cried. "You're not dead, after all!"

"Certainly I'm not dead!" answered the frog indignantly. "Why should I be dead? Dead, indeed! I'm in the prime of life."

"I'm sorry," said Dakin humbly. "Somebody told me you might help me, if only you weren't dead. So I'm very glad to meet you."

"Can't help you," said the frog at once. "Can't possibly help you. But I'm glad to meet you, too. Sit down, sit down. Have a fly."

There didn't seem anywhere to sit except on the floor, so Dakin sat there. Then she saw that Old Croak was holding out a large fly, which he apparently expected her to take.

"What—what am I to do with that?" she asked.

"Eat it, of course," croaked her host. "What else? Delicious! One of my last," he added sadly. "And who knows when there'll be any more? But never mind, I don't entertain often. Nothing but the best is good enough for the only visitor I've had in two hundred years."

Dakin naturally supposed he was exaggerating about the time. As to the fly, she didn't know what to say. She couldn't take the poor old thing's last one, especially when she didn't want it.

"Thank you very much," she said, "but as a matter of fact, I ate before I came. So why don't you have it?"

"Really?" asked the frog, his wrinkled old eyes lighting up. "Well, in that case—" He popped the fly into his wide mouth and gulped it down, beaming with pleasure.

"I suppose there aren't many flies around here," said Dakin.

"Hardly any," said Old Croak, shaking his head. "Windows sealed up, no door . . . They don't come down the chimney much. I suppose I shall starve to death one of these days. No doubt that's what she wants. No one will care." He heaved a deep, wheezy sigh and sat brooding on the lily leaf with his chin in his green hands.

"Who is 'she'?" Dakin ventured to ask.

The frog started and nearly fell into the water.

"Shhh!" he hissed warningly. He looked all around, and then beckoned her closer. She kneeled on the edge of the pool, and he hopped from one leaf to another until he was able to speak right into her ear.

"The witch!" he muttered.

Dakin grew cold. "A real witch?"

"Oh, she's real enough—by night, anyway," he added strangely.

"Have you ever seen her?" asked Dakin doubtfully. Of course there were plenty of stories about witches, but she wasn't prepared to believe unless there was some proof.

"Seen her? *Seen* her?" hissed Croak, his eyes popping. "I see her every night, *every night*, mark you! Down that chimney she comes, in her dark glasses and all her colored rags—for she's not one of your black witches, you know, color's the thing with her—and she reaches up to the ceiling and takes down her witch ball. Look! Do you see it hanging up there?"

Dakin looked at it again. Now that she knew it was a real witch's ball, not just a silver decoration, she realized how sinister it was with its strange greenish sheen.

"Lights up at night, you know," continued Croak in a hushed whisper. "That's how she searches, every night, hunting, hunting . . . through the woods, all over the mountain. Then at dawn she comes back. Hangs the ball up. Throws me a few curses (though I usually hide in the pool where it's safe). Takes herself off . . ."

"What is it she's looking for?"

"Ah! I could tell you—" He stopped and looked around again. "I daren't, though. Not with that thing hanging there. Not with her being the way she is during the day. I've heard she sleeps in a cave up there near the peak, but I don't believe it. I don't believe she ever sleeps! I—" He stopped again, and a look of terror came into his eyes. "Listen!" he whispered. "Can't you *hear*?"

Dakin listened. Everything had gone very quiet, the same kind of quiet as in the wood. Outside the murky window the sun had gone in and the cabin had grown suddenly so dark that Dakin could hardly see Old Croak at all. She swallowed fearfully and put out her hand. The frog gripped one finger with his little cold pads.

"Can't you *hear*?" he whispered again.

And now Dakin did hear. A terrible roaring, groaning, gnashing sound, faint at first, and then growing louder and louder, as if some dreadful creature was approaching, grumbling and talking to itself.

"What is it?" whispered Dakin in the darkness.

The frog had to swallow several times before he answered. "Drackamag," he gulped at last.

"But who—what—*is* Drackamag?" asked Dakin, as the terrifying noise got closer and closer.

4
DRACKAMAG

"SHHH!"

Now it was almost as dark as night, and the grumbling and roaring was right outside the window, sounding as thunder would sound if it were right next to your ear. It stopped for a moment, and then a deep, rumbling voice shouted down the chimney:

"Croak! Who have you got in there?"

"Don't speak!" muttered Old Croak hoarsely. "He's very stupid. If we don't speak, he may go away."

"I heard that!" roared Drackamag, and the vibrations made the lily pads rock like cockleshells on a rough sea. "Stupid, am I? We'll see who's stupid one of these days when I put my foot right down on this little house of yours, wait and see if I don't!"

Croak cowered down as if expecting the cabin to be crushed over his head at any moment.

"Come on, you ugly little lump of nothing! Who's in there? I heard someone laugh. Horrible! Frightened me out of my wits. No one's laughed on this side of the wood since . . . well, not for two hundred years, eh, Croak? We can't be having that sort of thing; it might lead to anything! Birds singing, bees humming—dangerous, *dangerous*, Croak! Eh? Eh?"

"You shouldn't have laughed," whispered the frog to Dakin in a shocked tone.

"Why not?" asked Dakin, feeling suddenly braver. If the simple sound of a laugh could frighten the terrible Drackamag, he couldn't be such a monster after all, however big he was.

"I heard a girl's voice!" exclaimed the thunderous voice outside. "She sounded *happy*! If you've got anybody *good* in there, Croak, I'm warning you . . . Madam won't like it! Now, send her out this minute, or I'll go and wake the old girl up and ask her if I can crunch your house down!"

Dakin stood up. Her legs shook a bit, but not too badly, considering.

"Don't go out!" whispered her friend frantically. "Let him do what he likes!"

"I'm not going out," Dakin assured him loudly. "I'm just going to laugh."

"No! NO! Not that!" howled the voice outside, and now the lily pads danced so wildly that Old Croak fell into the water with a splash.

But Dakin was already laughing and didn't notice. It wasn't any too easy to laugh, as there was nothing very funny about the situation; but it was important, so Dakin did it. She remembered the time Margle, her brother, had scoffed at the calf who fell into the mudhole and immediately afterward fallen in himself. She thought of the expression on the face of the hen when the chick she'd raised had turned out to be a duck and had hopped into the pond. She recalled the hornet-fly that wanted to sit on the pastor's nose last Sunday in the sermon. New laughter bubbled up in her with each thing she thought of, and soon the mere idea of the dreadful Drackamag being frightened was enough to keep her going.

Her laughter rang out, peal after joyful peal, until the crest of the mountain seemed to echo it back to her. But at last she was so tired, and her tummy ached so much, that she couldn't laugh anymore, and she sat down on the floor, too exhausted by her effort to make another sound.

She looked around. The first thing she noticed was that it was light again: The sun was shining in through the dusty window. Dakin realized that the sun hadn't really gone in, but that Drackamag's body had shut it out, like a black cloud. Birds outside were singing and all the sounds of a sweet summer noontime were pouring down the chimney like music. Drackamag and his fearful roaring voice were, for the moment, gone.

She looked for Old Croak and finally found him huddled behind a plant with his eyes tight shut and his pads in his ears. She tried to make him hear her, but of course he couldn't, so at last she gently touched him.

He leaped two feet clean into the air with fright, landed on the ground, and did a beautiful swallow dive into the pond, where he vanished, leaving only a bubble to show where he'd gone.

Dakin was alone again.

5
THE SPIKES

WELL, IT WAS TIME to be on her way. But there was one more thing she could do. Opening her knapsack, she took out the toffee and laid it in the fireplace at the foot of the chimney. Almost at once, a fly who happened to be passing overhead saw it and buzzed down to investigate. Then came another, and another. Old Croak would find a feast awaiting him when at last he had to surface for air.

Getting out of the chimney, Dakin discovered, was a different matter from getting in, and for a while it seemed she was doomed to stay there forever. But in trying to draw herself up, she accidentally touched a rough place in the bricks and a little rope ladder suddenly fell out of the inside rim of the chimney pot and dangled before her. In no time at all she was sliding down the sloping roof and clambering down the ladder into the sunny meadow again.

The meadow was wide, and as long as she was out in the sunshine she felt strangely safe. Could it be that whatever dark forces held the farthest-away mountain in their spell were as afraid of the light as they were of the happy sounds of laughter and birdsong? If so, then Dakin felt she might have discovered a very helpful secret in Old Croak's cabin.

But no meadow stretches forever and, quite abruptly, the grass stopped and she found herself walking on rocks: not the smooth, well-worn kind in the green river at home, but spiky, sticking-up rocks, like sharp teeth or knives. Her feet slipped between them and she had to wrench them free. Sometimes a piece of rock she hadn't noticed would trip her up. She knew if she fell she'd hurt herself badly, and it really did seem, after a while, as if the rocks were alive and doing their utmost to make her stumble and fall in among them.

Whenever she looked ahead, the jagged teeth, like the spears of a vast army, seemed to stretch for miles, ahead and on both sides; and even looking back, she couldn't see any sign of the meadow. The sun had really gone in now and the sky overhead was gray and threatening. She grew more and more weary, but there wasn't one friendly flat surface to rest on, just the endless, treacherous sea of spikes. It was no good turning back; she could only go on. It was worse than the wood.

At last Dakin grew so tired she knew that very soon she

must either sit down and rest, or fall down. Her head had begun to whirl and she realized she must be terribly hungry. Even without the little troll, her knapsack felt like lead, and her heart felt almost as heavy.

As she staggered on, she felt a lump come into her throat. First she told herself it was just tiredness, then, as it grew bigger, that it was hunger, but despite all her efforts to deceive herself, two big tears bloomed slowly on her lower eyelashes and made two wet, crooked paths down her brown cheeks.

They met on the end of her chin and fell with a small splash on a particularly spiteful-looking point of rock.

What happened next would have surprised Dakin if she hadn't already had more surprises that day than she knew how to deal with. The rock on which her tear had fallen began to melt, like a fast-burning wax candle. First the sharp point disappeared, then the thickening column beneath it sank and sank with a faint hissing sound, until it had quite melted away and there was nothing left but a flat place—exactly the size and shape of Dakin's foot.

Wrenching her scuffed boot from between two other spikes, she put it on this flat place. How lovely it was to rest it there! She stood on one leg. She had stopped crying, but another tear that had been on her cheek now slipped off and fell on another point of rock. The same thing happened as before: The sharp point melted, or at any rate quickly disappeared, and now there was a place for her other foot, and she was able to have quite a nice rest. But still ahead, behind, and all around her stretched an endless desert of other spikes, which Dakin didn't at all see how she would ever get through.

And then she had an idea.

"Aren't I silly!" she said aloud. "It was my *tears* that made the spikes go away. Tears must have power over the horrible rocks, just as laughter had power over Drackamag. Oh dear . . . but I don't feel a bit like crying now I've had a rest! What shall I do?"

After thinking a moment, she said, "Well. I didn't feel like laughing when Drackamag was outside the cabin, either. But I did it, because I had to. Now let's see if I can't make myself cry."

So she looked up at the miserable, gray sky and thought about how alone she was, how the little troll, her friend as she'd thought, had deserted her, about poor Old Croak, lonely, friendless, and afraid on his lily pad. She wasn't crying yet, but something was happening deep down inside her, so she made herself think about home, and how her mother would feel when she came down to make the breakfast and found her gone. She thought of her mother crying, of her father's face with all its lines showing plainly as they did when he was sad or angry, she thought of Triska, when night came and there was no one in the bed beside her. (Here it came! Oh, goodness, *floods*—had she overdone it?) She started to walk forward. The tears fell fast, and each one melted a spike so that she could move another step. Now she thought how *she* would feel tonight, without Triska, with no mother to kiss her and tuck her in—heavens! She couldn't see where she was going for tears! Thick and fast they fell, and her feet met only flat ground as she walked, and cried, faster and faster.

All of a sudden, she stumbled and fell. As she was falling, she had a horrible feeling that she was going to come down right onto one of the spikes, that it would stick into her. She flung her hands forward, expecting them to be grazed or even pierced by the sharp points, but—wonder of wonders! No such thing. She fell onto something quite soft.

Rubbing the last tears out of her eyes, she sat up and looked around. The spikes were nowhere to be seen. She was on a grassy path between two high walls of rock, far too steep for anyone to climb. The path led upward, around a corner. Picking herself up, she ran ahead. When she got around the bend, she stopped.

6
THE MOUNTAIN PATH

SHE WAS ON A ledge, high, high above a beautiful valley. The grassy path led away to the left, around the rock wall, out of sight. Unless she wanted to go back, she had no alternative to following this path. Ahead was a sheer drop of thousands of feet, and this drop would be on her right all the way along the path too. The path was narrow. She was quite an experienced climber, but she didn't like the look of it. She would have to watch her step very carefully along there.

Before she started she thought she had better eat something, so she sat down on the ledge and opened her knapsack. The bread and cheese tasted delicious. She only wished she'd brought an apple. And she hadn't thought about anything to drink. Lucky she'd left the toffee at the cabin; she would certainly have wanted to eat it, and it would only have made her thirstier than she was. If that were possible. . . . Goodness, how salty that cheese was! She'd never noticed before, but then, before there'd always been plenty of water in the pump, ice-cold, bubbling, crystal-clear water. . . . She swallowed, not that there was much *to* swallow. Her mouth felt as dry and shriveled up as an old bit of leather.

Still, there was nothing to be done about it, so when she'd packed up her knapsack again and got up, she started along the narrow path. It followed the sides of the mountain in bends and curves, all the time going upward. After a while it grew even narrower, so that Dakin had to flatten her front against the side of the rock and edge her way along sideways.

"It's lucky Margle taught me to climb," she thought, "and never to look down." She must be very high above the valley by now; it was a long time since she had looked. The sun was setting, and it was getting colder and colder—partly because she was getting higher. Her thirst got worse until she thought she couldn't stand it anymore. She didn't let herself think how frightened she was of falling, but she felt the ledge get narrower and narrower until only half the length of her feet fitted onto it, her heels hanging over the edge and her hands clinging to little ridges in the rock.

"I can't go on like this much longer," she suddenly

realized. "Soon it will be dark!" This was a fearful thought. What when night came? And she couldn't see to find handholds? She couldn't cling like a monkey to one place all night! What a fool she'd been to start this part of her journey when the day was nearly over! What a fool she'd been, perhaps, to leave home at all.

She edged her way around another bend, and now her eye was caught by the sun down below her. Half of it had already disappeared behind the horizon. The rest, half a big red ball, was giving out the last five minutes of light. All the valley was already in shadow. Most of the mountain was too. When she had edged around the next bend, she would be plunged into the beginnings of the night.

Suddenly she was panic-stricken. Margle had once warned her that if she looked down when she was on a high, narrow ledge, she might become too frightened to move. This happened to her now for the first time. She clung to the gigantic mountain wall until her fingers turned white. Her legs trembled under her; her breath came in gasps of terror.

"Oh, help me . . . somebody . . . help me!" she whispered.

"Certainly," said a voice above her head. "If you know the password."

7
THE GARGOYLES

DAKIN STARED UPWARD THROUGH the gathering darkness.
When she saw a wickedly grinning little stone face on a
long neck sticking out of the rock above her, it was lucky
her fingers were too stiff to open or she would have fallen
from shock.

"P-password?" she gasped.

"Yes, yes," said the stone head impatiently. "Hurry up,
you're going to fall backward at any minute."

"But I don't know it!" cried Dakin.

"Too bad, you'll have to die then," said the head with a
careless chuckle. "Fancy trying to climb up here without
it! Someone should have told you not to."

"I was warned," said Dakin miserably. "Oh, why didn't I
listen?"

"Who warned you?"

"A little brass troll we keep on our mantelpiece. He said—"

"A troll!" exclaimed the head in quite a different voice. "Tell me about him!"

But now the sun went down completely. An icy wind began to blow, making a low, whining sound around the crags, and Dakin knew that she had a few seconds at best before her hold gave way.

"Oh, please!" she begged. "Save me! I know what you are, you're a gargoyle, and one of the reasons I came was to see you! If you are cruel and wicked, it's only because you're sad! Save me, save me, I know you will!"

Looking into the evil, grinning face of the gargoyle as she spoke, she saw it suddenly change. All the upturned, gleeful lines cut into the stone turned downward. The mouth opened and a strange cry came out, like the moan of the wind:

"AAAAH . . ."

It was the saddest sound Dakin had ever heard.

"Aaaah," it moaned. "Little child, little wise child! You are the first—the only one who has ever understood. Hold on, hold on a little longer! Brave the fear and the cold wind of death! Go forward, till you come to my brothers, one after another, and say to them what you've said to me. Without the password I may not save you, but yet you *must not* die, for there has never come one like you and there will never come another. Go on, go on, go on!"

Dakin tried, but her hands would not move.

"I can't!" she cried. "My hands are frozen! Oh, I'm going to fall!"—for she felt her legs buckling.

The gargoyle seemed to slip down the face of the rock, and its neck grew longer. When it came near her head, it stretched its neck to one side and bent its face until its mouth was over her fingers. Then the neck stretched the other way, and the fingers of her left hand were brought back to life by the prickly breath.

"That is all that I, Og, dare to do," whispered the gargoyle into her ear. "Your hands will be warm and strong till you reach my brother, Vog, around the next bend. He will breathe on your knees to keep them stiff. Next you will come to my brother Zog. He will bring your feet back to life. After that . . . I don't know. But be strong for our sakes! Forgive me for making you afraid. . . . I could not help it! Go now, go quickly, for you are still in danger."

Dakin did not need to be told *that*, for although her hands were now warm and alive and she could move them along to find new holds, her legs were as weak, the path as narrow, the wind as cold, and the oncoming night as dark as ever—and she was still almost paralyzed with fear. But something in the gargoyle's voice—something pleading, frantic almost—gave her new hope and strength. "It must be knowing that I've come here for a *reason*, not just out of a stubborn fancy," thought Dakin. "Though what the reason is, I still don't know." And with a great effort she began to edge her way forward again.

Now she had to climb mainly by touch. Her hands, though, seemed to have eyes of their own and her fingers found places to hold on to that her real eyes couldn't see. When her knees gave way, her hands took a firm grip on the ridges of rock and held up her whole body until her knees felt stronger and she was able to go on.

As she rounded the next bend she called out loudly, "Vog! Vog! Are you there?"

"Shhh!" hissed a voice somewhere low down on the rock wall. "Who calls me by my name? Who raises his voice in this dread place?"

"I'm a her, not a him. My name is Dakin. Your brother Og said you'd help me because I know that gargoyles are only wicked because they're sad."

"Ahhh!"

It was the same mournful moan as before.

"How do you know this secret of secrets?" asked Vog.

"I saw pictures in a book about churches," panted Dakin. "All the gargoyles in the pictures looked like evil spirits, but their stone eyes seemed to me to be full of sorrow."

"And have you never heard that you will turn to stone if you look at one?"

"Yes, my mother said so. But it can't be true."

"It is true."

"But I looked your brother Og in the face, and I didn't turn to stone!"

"Perhaps you were like stone already?"

"Oh yes, of course! From fear of falling. Did that save me?"

"That, and your own knowledge of us . . . What did Og say I was to do?"

"Blow on my knees."

"Why? Only give the password and I can lift you from the path."

"I don't know it."

"Oh woe!" cried Vog. "Then we are all doomed! For without the password you will never get past the Colored Snow Witch who guards the snow line. And unless you get past her, you cannot reach the top."

"Well, we'll see," said Dakin. "I've got this far. Now, blow on my knees, or they won't hold me until I reach your brother Zog."

So Vog blew the same prickly breath onto her knees, and immediately Dakin felt them take on new strength. Though her feet were now so cold that she couldn't feel them, somehow she made herself go forward, and very soon she heard a voice, even lower, right on a level with the path, cry out:

"Beware, beware, you will break my long neck with your great clumsy feet! One more step and you fall to your doom!" and the horrible, wicked chuckle of a gargoyle who did not yet know that Dakin understood him.

"You're not really bad enough to laugh at the thought of me falling," she said through the darkness. "You've been made bad through sadness."

"Ahhhh!"

"Yes, ahhhh," she said, a bit impatiently. "Now, Zog, breathe on my poor cold feet and tell me what to do next."

It was really lovely to feel her feet coming back to life, like climbing into a warm bed after a long walk through the snow.

"Oh, thank you, Zog, that's so much better," she said. "Well! I wish one of you would blow on my eyes so that I could see in the dark, that's all, and perhaps give me a drink, and then I'd be ready for anything, even Dracka-mag and the Colored Snow Witch."

Zog let out a hiss like a snake (and indeed, a gargoyle with its long neck is not unlike a snake with a goblin's head). The hiss seemed to rise upward until it was above her head.

"The eyes I cannot manage," came Zog's voice. "But as to the drink: Even down below where humans live and our kind have no life, water still pours out of our mouths. Put back your head, child of wisdom and mystery, and open your lips."

Dakin did this, and a moment later a delicate stream of clear cold water ran into her mouth and down her throat as fast as she could gulp.

Whether there was something magic about the water or not she didn't know, but she suddenly felt not only warmer and stronger, but much braver as well.

"Oh, Zog, you are a good gargoyle!" she cried.

"Ahhhh—"

"Never mind that," she interrupted quickly. "Now, give me your advice. What lies ahead? What must I do?"

"I know nothing," said Zog. "We, my brothers and I, are only sentinels. Those whom the great Drackamag wishes to pass hold the password; others we are ordered to let fall to their deaths."

"Drackamag is wicked, isn't he? I mean, really wicked, not like you?"

"Wicked! Aye, wicked, wicked as a witch's claws, wicked as an ogre's fang!"

"Then I suppose that the only visitors he would want to see must be wicked too. He wouldn't want *good* people coming up here; I mean people who wanted to help you and Old Croak, for instance."

The moaning voice of Zog changed suddenly into a much more normal, friendly tone, almost like a person's voice.

"You have seen Croak? He is still alive? Oh, tell me about him, tell me about the warm, sweet world of the meadow! Do the flowers still grow there, do the birds still sing? Is it all as it was so long ago?"

"Yes, it's all beautiful. Especially after walking through that hateful wood. And old Croak is very nice, but he seems afraid."

"We are all afraid—all of us," said Zog, moaning again. "But tell me more. Is the Lithy Pool still there in the midst of the meadow, with its sweet magic waters?"

Dakin felt herself grow cold again with a different kind of fear. "Lithy Pool? What Lithy Pool? There was no pool in the meadow!" she said. If she had missed bathing in the Lithy Pool! The troll had said she must.

Zog seemed puzzled. "Has Drackamag then destroyed that well of wonders?" he asked. "I know he would if he could, but I dared hope he had not the power. . . . Yet if the Lithy Pool is gone, how could Croak live? For as I heard, he is still a frog, and frogs cannot live without a pond."

"A *pond*?" exclaimed Dakin. "Oh yes, he has a pond. It's inside a sort of a little house. But that can't be the—" She stopped. Then, in a voice hushed with uneasiness, she went on: "Don't tell me *that pond* is the Lithy Pool?"

"There is but one, right in the middle of the meadow. It has lilies growing on it, and it is very deep. Some say it goes down to the middle of the earth, and all who bathe in it are protected from the powers of evil."

"Oh no, oh no!" thought Dakin. "That means I've got to go all the way back . . . down the path, across those awful spikes . . . hours and hours! I can't do it, I simply can't!" Aloud to Zog, she said, "The troll said I should bathe in the Lithy Pool. Do you think it's important enough to go back for?"

"It depends on whether you want to live or die," said Zog. "If you are an ordinary human child, without magic on your side, I do not see how you have reached *here* without having bathed in the Lithy Pool. It's impossible that you should reach the top of the mountain without some special protection. What troll?" he asked suddenly, as if he'd only just realized what she'd said.

"A little brass troll my father found on the far edge of the wood," she said.

"Where is he? Where did you see him?" Zog asked with what sounded like excitement.

"I brought him from home, but in the wood he came alive, and ran away when he heard where I was going."

"So he would, so he would indeed!" said Zog. "If Drackamag ever lays claws on him again, he'll melt him down and make a brass button out of him for his waist-coat!"

"Why? What's he done?"

"He stole something very important."

"What is it?"

"I can't tell you—I dare not."

"Oh well, I can't bother about that now. I can't hang on here all night. Is there nowhere I can lie down and rest, Zog? Surely you can tell me that."

"What is wrong with here?"

"But this ledge is too narrow to stand on, much less lie on!"

"Move along a little to your right."

Dakin did this, and suddenly, for the first time for hours, her heels were on solid ground. She carefully felt about with her feet and found herself standing on a broad ledge. It even had some dry grass on it to make it softer. She sank down with great relief, put her knapsack under her head for a pillow, and almost at once felt herself falling off to sleep.

"Good night, dear Zog," she said. "In the morning I'll think what to do. Will you guard me in the night?"

"Aye. Don't fear."

Dakin drew her warm cloak around her and fell asleep instantly.

8
THE TUNNEL

WHEN SHE WOKE, THE sun was up, but on the other side of the mountain, so that her ledge was still in shadow. But she was not cold. Zog must have been breathing on her in the night, because she could feel the icy wind blowing on her, yet she didn't get chilled by it.

At once she looked around for her gargoyle friend. She was very touched to see that he had moved around to the edge of the ledge, where he had curved his long neck upward into a kind of stone hook, to stop her from rolling off in her sleep. He was staring out across the valley, far below, where the vast pointed shadow of the mountain fell across rivers, fields, and villages like a witch's hat.

Dakin laid her hand gently on his stone head.

"Good morning, Zog," she said.

Zog started as if in fright when she touched him, but then he seemed to push up against her hand like a cat being stroked, and she knew he was going to start moaning, "Ahhhh," again, as all the gargoyles did when she was kind to them, so she quickly said, "Now I must eat some breakfast and think about what I'm to do."

"Yes," said Zog. "You must not delay. Drackamag sleeps late, but the witch is still about until the sun falls on her. She is a night creature, of course."

"And Drackamag is a day creature?" asked Dakin, munching bread and cheese.

"Oh yes, he's not a specter. He is all too real."

"What is he?"

Zog stared at her. "Do you not even know that?"

"No."

"He is an ogre. One of the biggest in the world."

Dakin swallowed hard. "Oh." Her mouth was suddenly too dry to eat. "Could I have another drink, please?" she asked in a small voice.

Zog glided along the rock face until he was above her, and then opened his mouth and trickled water into hers. She thought he had a dear little face now that he didn't look wicked anymore, and she patted it when she had drunk her fill.

"Thank you, Zog. You're so sweet."

"Ahhhh—," he groaned dolefully.

"Now, don't start that! Everything's going to be all

right. I don't think I'll bother about the Lithy Pool, though I do wish I'd known what it was at the time. Are there any other hints you can give me?"

"When you arrive at the snow line, wait until the sun is shining where you are. The Colored Snow Witch will be asleep then. When you're walking through the snow, be sure only to walk where it's white. The colors are not natural, they're the work of the Colored Snow Witch, who stains them with great splashes of dye from her caldron. They have their own evil magic. Then there's the Winged One."

Dakin dropped her last piece of cheese, and it rolled to the edge and fell down, down, down—lost forever.

"The *what*?" she gasped in horror.

"It is a flying monster," said Zog. "It lives in a cave, just below the summit of the mountain. It's Drackamag's watchdog, his slave. I don't know what you can do to save yourself from *that*, if you're not willing to go back and bathe in the—"

Just at that moment, a faint trembling went through the very rock of the mountain. Zog stopped talking and a look of terror came over his face.

"It's him!" he whispered. "He's making his morning rounds early! Oh, do go on. If he catches you here near me, he'll break me off and throw me down the mountain and I'll be smashed to a thousand pieces! Hurry ahead, you'll find a cave just around the corner with a tunnel . . . too small for him. Good luck . . . be brave—now go! Do go!"

The vibrations were getting stronger, and now Dakin could hear the thunderous muttering she had heard in the cabin when Drackamag was coming. Giving Zog a very quick kiss and then stifling his "Ahhhh—" with her hand, she picked up her knapsack and ran nimbly along the path, which, where it led off from her sleeping ledge, was much wider than before.

As the thunder and the shaking increased, she rounded a corner and saw the cave before her. It was quite small, a little round hole in the wall, just about big enough for her to crawl into. This she did, and only just in time, for at once the mouth of her cave grew dark as a huge hand passed in front of it.

Drackamag, it seemed, was lying somewhere above, and feeling with his huge fingers along all the ledges to make sure no one was on them. The hole into which Dakin had crawled was big enough to let in only Drackamag's little finger—if you could call that great thing like a pink tree-trunk little—and now in it came, poking about to see if anyone was in there. Dakin crept backward, staying out of its reach. Heavens, how big the whole of him must be! The little light that still came in around the root of his finger showed the most horrible nail she had ever seen—a great curved horny claw. She simply shivered with horror as this awful thing wiggled in front of her, but she knew not one more inch of Drackamag could get in, and there was plenty of tunnel behind her, so for the moment she was safe enough.

At last Drackamag's finger was taken out of the cave, and then she heard his voice roaring:

"Zog! Vog! Og! What have you to report?"

She heard Zog's voice, very near, calling back, "Nothing, sir!" and then two other voices, each a little fainter, echoing: "Nothing, sir!" "Nothing, sir!" Drackamag muttered and grumbled a bit and then said, in tones that made the mountain tremble, "Graw thought he smelled something in the night—*human flesh*, lads, human flesh! What do you say to that, eh? And yesterday I could have sworn I heard someone *laugh*, down in the meadow. I warned Croak, and now I'm warning you . . . if there's any treachery, heads will roll—stone heads—you get it? They'll roll a long, long way!" Then Drackamag gave vent to a really fearful roar, so loud that bits of rock from the roof of Dakin's cave broke off and came tumbling down.

Then it seemed that Drackamag must have gone off to another part of the mountain, for the trembling grew less and everything got quiet. Dakin was just going to venture out, when she thought perhaps she would try following the tunnel for a little way to see where it took her. She would be much safer in here—who knew when Drackamag would make his rounds again?

So she crawled and crawled, right into the mountain itself. It was pitch dark, of course, after the tunnel turned its first corner, but Dakin remembered that she'd put a candle and some matches in her knapsack, and soon she had a friendly little light to help her find the way.

The tunnel was all ice-cold stone, and her knees and elbows were soon sore from crawling along. The tunnel led all the time up and up, getting steeper and steeper, until at last Dakin was climbing rather than crawling and had to put the candle out and away because she needed both hands. It seemed her hands and feet still had some magic left in them from the gargoyle's breath, because they found holds even in the dark, and soon Dakin could see a bright point of light far above her. She climbed eagerly toward it.

9
THE PAINTED SNOW

IN A FEW MORE minutes her head and shoulders came out into brilliant sunlight. The glare was too much for her eyes after the darkness and she had to close them at first, but gradually she peeped through her eyelashes and saw that part of the reason for the brightness was that she was high above the snow line. All around her was snow. She knew it was snow because of the cold, but it was very odd, just the same. The Colored Snow Witch had clearly been hard at work here. All the ground looked like a piece of paper on which some child, without the least idea of colors, had been playing with paints—a bad-tempered child, rubbing and scrubbing with his brush and pouring daubs of paint here and there at random. It really looked unpleasant, especially to Dakin, who was used to the shining, pure white of the valley snow in winter and did not like all these out-of-place purples and reds and oranges where they did not belong.

She looked about her. There was no one—no *thing*—in sight, only the wild, clashing colors, all glinting evilly in the sun. She searched the slopes for a patch of white and at last she saw a very small triangle, like a bit of white paper that the child has, quite by accident, forgotten to color. But it was at least ten steps up the mountainside from the mouth of her cave. How would she reach it?

She saw no other way than by just wading through to it. Zog had warned her about the colored snow, but he hadn't actually told her not to walk on it. She pushed her knapsack out first and dumped it onto a patch of green snow, then pulled herself out. There was no snow on the very rim of the cave, so she sat there to put on her knapsack. But when she picked it up, she caught sight of something on the bottom of it that made her drop it again very quickly.

Every part that had touched the snow was crawling with green caterpillars.

Now, it wasn't that Dakin minded caterpillars in the ordinary way. But these were not ordinary caterpillars, such as you find on cabbage leaves. These were big, sluglike things, slimy-looking, and, Dakin suddenly saw, they had small but busy jaws, munching, munching—

"Heavens, they're eating my knapsack!"

Holding it up by the straps, she banged it hard against a rock to shake the witchy creatures off. They fell off, all right, and disappeared at once into the snow. But the whole bottom of Dakin's knapsack was gone—eaten by them in a few seconds—and everything that was left in it tumbled out and fell into the snow, too. She just about managed to grab the book of poems before it disappeared.

The snow everything fell into was a blazing red, and when Dakin tried to reach into it to recover the bread, the candles, and the knife and mug, she snatched her hand away. Have you ever touched what they call "dry ice"? It is so cold it feels red hot. And this is how the red snow felt. Dakin could not touch it.

She could have cried when she examined her knapsack, or what was left of it. It was impossible to put anything into it now—it was like an upside-down bag with a couple of straps attached, No food, no candle, nothing! Well . . . but at least she had the poems. . . . She opened the book and read one to cheer herself up a little.

> *Child of wisdom, child of courage,*
> *You are nearer than you know,*
> *Underneath the ugly colors*
> *Seek and find the honest snow.*

"That's very funny," thought Dakin. "I thought I knew every poem in this book, but I don't remember that one." She wanted to read it again, but having taken her eyes off it for a moment, now, when she looked down at the page, she couldn't find it again. Wait a minute, how did it go? "Child of wisdom, child of courage . . ." "Oh, pooh to all that," thought Dakin, who had no conceit. "Nearer than you know." To what? To the summit, perhaps! Oh, what was the rest? Suddenly she remembered. Of course! The witch's colors would only be on the surface of the snow. The proper, white stuff must be underneath!

She stood up and with the toe of her boot gave the red patch of snow a sudden kick. It was like putting your finger very quickly through a candle flame—it didn't burn. The red snow scattered, and underneath lay whiteness. Ahead lay a purple patch, like a big splash of poison. "Whee!" cried Dakin and, sticking the toe of the other boot under the edge of it, sent it flying upward in a scurry of glittering violet crystals.

From then on, it was not only easy, but fun. She walked boldly forward, kicking the colored snow aside, until she stood safe on the island of white. Behind her lay ten white boot prints through five different colors.

"I've done it, I've done it!" she shouted. She turned again to face upward. The colored snow stretched ahead of her, but she feared nothing from it now. But above that loomed a tall, jutting rock that looked like a rough sort of castle. It stood straight up from the top of the snow, black, high, forbidding. "It must be the summit," she thought, and her blood froze. Because just where the door would be, if it had been a real castle, was a vast black cave.

All this happened while the echoes of her foolish shout of triumph were still booming around the crags—"Done it! Done it!" There was a moment's silence, even deeper and more frightening than the silence of the Wicked Wood. And then she heard a sound that turned her heart to ice.

10
CRAW

IT WAS A WILD and terrible cry, not the sort of cry we ever hear in the world now, but something from the far past, before there were any men on the earth, when weird and fearful creatures had it all to themselves. Then came something even worse: the slow, low whistling sound of great leathery wings beginning to beat.

"It's the flying monster!" thought Dakin, rooted to the ground with terror.

And so it was.

Out of the black mouth of the castle cave it came, flying very slowly and deliberately, twisting its great, horned head from side to side, with its wicked eyes catching the sunlight and throwing off sparks of light. One look at its face told Dakin at once that here was no poor good-hearted creature like the gargoyles, imprisoned by some evil spell in an ugly body—here was the evil itself! Its enormous, narrow wings, black and shiny like those of some gigantic black bat, sighed through the air, as if it were in no hurry, for no prey could escape it.

But the most awful part about it was its great, hooked talons. These hung down under its huge hairless, featherless body, and every few seconds, as it flew, they opened and closed, as if getting ready to—

Ah! It had seen her.

It turned, wheeling, and swooped toward her, with its spearlike beak pointing straight at her, its terrible eyes glaring. Dakin turned too, and tried to run, but she forgot about the colored snow. As soon as she stepped onto a big, mustard-yellow area, she stuck fast—the snow held her like tar—and she couldn't run! It was like the most terrible nightmare in the world. It was coming—its great black shadow was over her—and now—and now!

It was picking her up—yes—lifting her up in its terrible claws! Luckily the sharp talons only caught her cloak. It lifted her clear out of her boots. Dakin felt the icy air on her bare feet as she was whisked higher and higher into the sky. She closed her eyes tight, wondering why she didn't just die of fright and have done with it. After a while, though, when nothing else happened—that's to say, the dreadful creature neither dropped her nor ate her but

simply flew through the air with her—she cautiously opened them.

She quickly closed them again after a glimpse of the ground, far below, but curiosity soon got the better of her again. She actually managed to look around this time. The monster was carrying her down the slopes of the mountain. The colored snow was left behind, and now they were flying over a wide, gray area that looked like a desert. Of course, that would be the sea of spikes! And now, looking downward and ahead, she saw the sudden lovely green garden of the meadow, with Old Croak's cabin right in the middle of it.

In a matter of moments, the creature had brought her right back to the place it had taken her nearly a whole day to climb up from!

Oh, it was too bad! Dakin forgot to be frightened. All that walking, all that climbing, all that cold and thirst and being frightened! She'd teach that horrible, rotten monster to leave her alone!

She began to jump and struggle. She reached above her head and took hold of one of the talons that was locked in the strong folds of her cloak. She pulled herself up by it until her face was level with its black, bony leg. Then she bit it as hard as she could.

The creature let out a shrill squawk of pain and surprise, and would have dropped her, but she hung on. It swooped low, flexing its claws, trying to fling her off. It made awkward passes at her with its beak, but because she was underneath it, it couldn't see her.

And now they were right above the cabin. The monster was hovering in the air, trying to get at her. Looking down, she saw the chimney opening right below, not more than a few feet away. Quickly she tore the buttons off her cloak, and in another second she was falling free.

11
CROAK AGAIN

WHOOSH! DOWN THE CHIMNEY she dropped, as smoothly as a letter falling into a letter box. As she landed in the fireplace, she heard the clash of the monster's talons, clawing at the roof, and saw its shadow flash across the dusty window. Its angry cries circled the cabin once or twice, then faded away back up the mountain.

Breathing hard, Dakin looked around. Everything was exactly as she'd last seen it. There was the pool in the middle, with the lily pads and—oh joy!—there was dear Old Croak sitting on one of them, with his fingers in his ear holes and his eyes screwed shut.

Dakin was taking no chances this time. Creeping up to him very quietly, she reached her hand out and gently but firmly caught him in it. He jumped and quivered, but she held him, and after a moment he cautiously peeped at her. Then he took his fingers out of his ears at once.

"Oh, it's *you*!" he said, in tremendous relief. "I thought—I heard—oh dear, oh dear! What a terrible fright I got!" And he lay down on his back in her hand, his hands clasped to his chest, palpitating all over.

"Now, Croaky dear," said Dakin firmly, "there's no need to carry on like that. Nothing can get in here; surely you've found that out. Now do sit up, because I want to talk to you. Here, have a nice fly. You'll feel much better."

The cabin was abuzz with them. She caught one easily as it blundered against the windowpane, and popped it into Croak's open mouth. He gulped it down and immediately sat up.

"What a kind little miss you are, to be sure!" he said. "I'm so glad to see you again! Of course I knew you wouldn't get far, but I didn't think you'd ever actually come *back*. I cried

a lot about you, after you went, you know. Quite sure you'd be killed. . . . Well, never mind. So you decided to be sensible after all, then, and not go on?"

"Of course I went on," said Dakin indignantly. "And I did get far. I got to within sight of the summit, as a matter of fact—"

Old Croak's eyes popped. "You got *where*?"

"Nearly up to that big rock like an ogre's castle."

"What do you mean, *like* an ogre's castle?" cried Croak, jumping about in excitement. "It *is* an ogre's castle! It's Drackamag's castle, you foolish, rash little girl! Oh my goodness gracious me! And what about the spikes? And the witch? And her snow? And WHAT about the Gargoyle brothers? Oh, I can hardly believe it! Right to the top, she got! Oh, tell me, tell me everything; I can't wait to hear!"

He had fallen off her hand and was jumping about madly all over the cabin, tumbling into the pond every now and then and jumping out again. "Do sit still, Croaky!" said Dakin. "How can I talk to you when you're bouncing about like that? I promise I'll go away without telling you a thing if you don't stop it!" So in the end the frog had to sit still on the palm of her hand while she told him all her adventures, right from the very beginning— even the part about wanting a prince as her husband.

He was certainly a most wonderful audience, except that he kept interrupting with exclamations: "Good heavens!" "Fancy you guessing that!" "And what did he say?" "And how did you get out of that?" "Oh my goodness *gracious* me!" The end part, about the Winged One carrying her off, had him absolutely on the edge of her hand with suspense, with his eyes wide and both his tiny hands in his mouth.

"Oh, I do think you're brave! Oh, I *do* think you're brave!" he said at last. "You wonderful girl! Oh, you did deserve to get there, you did, you did!" He was nearly in tears. "It's too bad, that rotten Graw coming out and spoiling the end of the story!"

"But it's not the end," said Dakin.

"What?"

"It's not the end; how could it be?" said Dakin. "I haven't solved any of the mystery yet. I don't know why the mountain called me. I haven't helped the gargoyles. And there's that awful ogre, still up there, frightening everybody, not to mention the witch and Graw, as you call the brute. Ooh, don't I owe that Graw something, for bringing me down here again! Just wait till I catch him! Because now I've got to climb all the way up again, and even though I do know some of the secrets now, it's still an awfully long way."

Old Croak sat there staring at her for a long time.

"You're going back up there?" he asked at last.

"Of course," said Dakin.

Croak flopped off her hand and jumped slowly across the cabin and back, muttering to himself: "Never would have believed it. Never saw anything like it. Such determination. Such courage. Amazing. Amazing." Dakin, knowing he must mean her, tried not to listen. After a while she said:

"Though now I think about it, there is one good thing about coming back here again, and that is that now I can bathe in the pool. This *is* the Lithy Pool, isn't it?"

"The what? Oh yes—yes, of course. Go ahead, my dear. Help yourself. Very welcome, I'm sure."

Dakin didn't fancy getting herself all wet, but it couldn't be avoided, so she sat on the edge of the pool with her legs dangling in (the water was surprisingly warm), took the book out of her pocket, and then slipped in. Her feet didn't touch the bottom. She swam around once—it took about half a minute—and then pulled herself out again.

"Now go outside," said Croak. "Run about the meadow and get dry. Can't have you catching cold, can we? That would never do."

He was looking at her with a very strange expression on his froggy face. She was about to get the rope ladder down to climb out when he suddenly said:

"Just a minute."

She turned.

"One or two small things before you go."

"Yes?"

"Well, first of all, I'm not really a frog."

"If you're not a frog, what are you?"

"I don't know. No, don't laugh. It's true. I've forgotten what I once was. A man of some kind, probably, since I still have the gift of speech."

"But who changed you? Drackamag?"

"No, no, no, of course not! Drackamag's an ogre, not a

wizard. He can't do things like that. He's just a huge giant: a brute, a lout, and a bully. And the witch herself is harmless: She puts all her witchcraft into her colors, and the only thing she's afraid of is white."

"So who could it have been? Not the gargoyles . . . I won't believe that!"

"No, not them of course. They're as much victims as I am."

"Are there any other witches up there?"

"I believe not. I've never heard of any."

"So there's someone—or something—else, some—some wicked force behind all this."

"That has always been my idea."

They were silent for a moment, looking at each other.

"I must go and get dry," said Dakin. "I'm shivering." She started to go, then turned back once more and kissed the frog. It was as if she knew she wouldn't be coming back.

12
UP THE MOUNTAIN

OUT IN THE MEADOW she raced back and forth for a while. The sun and wind dried her so quickly that she realized the water was magic. What had Zog told her about it? That it had the power to repel evil. . . . In that case, she had nothing to worry about, other than natural accidents, such as falling down a mountain, for instance. . . .

Suddenly a white something caught her eye on the edge of the wood. She ran up to the trees. High on a branch she saw her stocking cap.

"I must get that back," she thought. "I really must."

The tree itself, which had stolen the cap from her head, as she supposed, was impossible to climb. But the one next to it was not so bad. After a long, tiring struggle,

Dakin managed to get nearly to the top of it and, by reaching over, was just able to get her hand on the white woolen cap. It was another matter to pull it free, for the tree it was caught in seemed to be holding on to it. Twice Dakin nearly fell, but at last she wrenched it off and, with one arm around the trunk of her tree, fit it securely onto her head.

She had been so much occupied, she hadn't noticed that her struggle in the treetops had been seen by sharp eyes far away. But now a heavy dark shadow fell on her, a shadow that filled her with a far-from-ordinary chill. Her face snapped up. Yes! It was Graw, swooping close above her, his dreadful claws opening to snatch her again!

"Ah ha!" thought Dakin, even as the shadow fell on her. "Now I've bathed in the Lithy Pool, you won't be able to harm me!" But she was in for a shock. Either the Lithy Pool water didn't work, or something else was wrong, because no sooner had she thought this than the great creature clamped his claws on her shoulders and flew off with her again.

Dakin started to scream as she felt the claws, but then she stopped, because although they seemed to be digging into her, she suddenly realized they weren't hurting. She felt herself firmly held, and when she looked, she could see the terrible claw nails, as sharp as daggers, pressing through her clothes; but they certainly weren't going through her skin.

"Maybe that's what the Lithy Pool does," she thought,

as well as she *could* think for the wind whipping her hair around her face and snatching breath out of her mouth. "It may be like a magic suit of armor that stops you actually getting hurt if someone tries to hit you or shoot an arrow at you or something. But I see it doesn't stop monsters from picking you up. Well," she added to herself, "perhaps it's not such a bad thing, if only it doesn't drop me! Because it's taking me straight up the mountain again to the lair of its master, Drackamag, which is where I wanted to go in any case, and it's saving me all that long climb."

It was all very well to be so calm about it and look on the bright side and so forth, but when the great, dark, rocky bulk of Drackamag's castle (which was the summit of the mountain) loomed ahead of her and the terrible Graw began circling it in great sweeps, Dakin began to get very frightened indeed. It really was a most awful-looking place. The turrets of the castle were no more than pinnacles of rock, which had been hollowed out from inside and rough windows cut through; these looked like so many caves (they weren't proper square windows) so that if you didn't know, you wouldn't think it was an ogre's castle at all. But flying close around them like this, Dakin could peep in as they passed one of these openings; and inside she could see cavelike rooms with huge bits of rough furniture, tables, and chairs, the legs of which were whole tree trunks and the tops like the decks of ships, a candle so thick Dakin couldn't have got her arms around it, and in the kitchen, a fireplace as big as Dakin's whole house, half filled with "twigs" that were the tops of trees, and a black cook pot in which you could have cooked a couple of bullocks without even chopping them up first.

All these rooms were dark and gloomy and Dakin thought with horror that she might soon find herself inside, in the power of Drackamag. She could have wished herself safely at home, and she certainly would have done had she not met the gargoyle brothers and Old Croak, who needed help so badly. How she could possibly help them she had no idea, but all of them had said that she could, and after all—the mountain had called her.

She had no more time to think about it now, though, because Graw had reached the front of the castle for the third time around and was now flying with her into the vast mouth of the cave door.

It was dark in there, so dark that Dakin kept blinking to make sure her eyes were really open. Graw flapped slowly on, until they must have been right in the heart of the mountaintop. Then, quite suddenly, just when she least expected it—he dropped her.

13
THE BLUE BEAD

THE FALL WAS HORRIBLE but short. She landed on a hard stone floor. For a moment she lay still, stunned, but only by fright: The magic of the Lithy Pool had protected her from every other hurt but that.

"I really must try to be a bit braver," thought Dakin as she sat up, "especially now. I must *trust* the Lithy Pool water."

She stood up. It was still perfectly dark. She could sense that she was in a huge, very high cave; she knew this by the way every little sound she made echoed. Also, she could still hear Graw, his wings making their uncanny whistling sound and his beak clacking, high, high above her.

And now she heard another sound. Actually, she felt it

first, in the stone under her feet: the trembling of the mountain as Drackamag walked. She fumbled in her pocket and found the troll's little blue bead, or sweet, or whatever it was, and popped it into her mouth. It had a strong, rather disgusting but healthy sort of taste, like disinfectant. Now she could see that the cave was growing lighter. A flickering light spread across the great rocky rough-cut walls. Thud, thud, thud—and with each footfall the light of the giant candle drew nearer and lit up more of the cave, as the ogre came along a vast passage toward her.

"I don't suppose," thought Dakin, trying not to shake, "that the magic water could protect me if Drackamag actually stood on me, so I'd better run and stand against a wall, not here in the middle of the floor!" She quickly did this, but Graw, hovering above in the eerie blackness, saw her run and, thinking she was trying to escape, swooped down on her with a harsh cry. She ducked into a crevice of the rock, and the tip of his black wing just brushed her face as it wheeled by with a swish of air like a sword stroke.

"Ugh!" Dakin exclaimed. Its wing had a horrid smell, like something dead. Dakin put up her hand to wipe away the cold, cold touch from her face—and got the shock of her life.

Her hand was transparent.

Even as she stared at it, it faded altogether and disappeared.

For a second Dakin thought—well, it would be hard to describe her thoughts. Had she gone blind? But no, the walls of the great cave were still clear before her, clearer and clearer, in fact, as the ogre's candle approached. How then could she not be able to see her hand right before her face?

She looked down at herself. But there was no herself. She was there—she could breathe, she could feel the cold floor under her bare feet, she could touch her face and hair and feel them warm and real—yet she was *not* there, for she could not see any part of her body or clothes.

Suddenly she understood. The troll's blue sweet, which he had told her would protect her from Drackamag, had made her invisible.

But she had no time to think any more about it, because now Drackamag himself had come into the cave. He was so huge that she couldn't see him properly. One of his great booted feet thundered down right outside her crevice: She could have reached out and touched the side of it, but she was only as tall as the *sole* of the boot. She could look up and see part of the rest of it, but not much more than that. The ogre himself nearly filled the whole of the cave, and when he spoke, no thunder that ever rocked Dakin's house on a stormy night had ever sounded half so loud and boomy. She had to put her fingers hard in her ears to prevent herself being deafened by the vibrations, and still she could hear his words quite clearly.

"Did you get her, Graw? Where is she?"

The Winged One squawked shrilly and tried, perhaps, to fly down to where Dakin was hiding, but Drackamag's enormous bulk blocked the way.

"Well, don't just flap about around my face, you stupid brute!" roared the ogre. "Show me, can't you? Oh, if the Master is clever enough to bring a thing like you back to life, couldn't he manage to make you talk, too? He gave *me* a voice, and a brain, and a bit of sense in my—OWWCH!"

Dakin felt the whole mountain jar. It was like an earthquake. She fell over. She guessed Drackamag must have bumped his head on the roof of the cave.

"And come to that, why didn't the Master make these caves bigger before he put me into them?" he roared. "That's the third time in two days I've banged my head! The whole lot'll come crashing down one of these times, crashing right down, you'll see! Then where will the Master be? Lost in the rubble, and serve him right! Serve him right. Come here, you, stop digging your stupid talons into my shoulder; can't you see I'm stuck? Wait a minute, I'll sit down."

There was a lot of heaving and grunting and puffing; several bits of rock—boulders, really—came tumbling down, and again the whole mountain seemed to shudder and shake. The light, which had been partly blocked off, now became brighter, and when Dakin looked out of her crevice she saw, instead of the side of the ogre's boot, a vast area of coarse green cloth, which must have been a bit of Drackamag's trousers. He was sitting down on the floor, and now Graw was swooping about, making horrible shadows in the flickering light of the giant candle, still trying to get down to where Dakin was.

But it seemed the ogre hadn't got a very good memory, or maybe his knock on the head had made him forget about Dakin. For instead of looking for her, he caught Graw in his hand and said:

"Now keep still, you brainless bird or lizard or whatever you are; you're getting on my nerves, bashing around me like that. I want to think. Oww, my head! How I hate this job. . . . If you don't stop trying to peck me, I'll give you such a thick ear! Wonder when the Master'll be back. . . . Always off looking for that stupid ring . . . as if it mattered! If Prince Rally can't be married without it, as if I cared about *that*, and it's lost, then what does it matter if the troll has it or the Master has it or if it's at the bottom of the Lithy Pool? I bet that's where it is, if you ask me. And even *he* can't get it out of there." The ogre gave a chuckle. "Ho, ho! Wouldn't I like to see him try! Even I had to build a house around it because I couldn't stand the sight of it, and I'm not half as bad as he is! I bet he'd burst into a million pieces if he so much as dipped his little finger into it, and if he jumped in to look for the ring—wow! He'd just go up in a puff of steam! Poof, Graw, poof! A couple of bubbles—that'd be the Master. You wouldn't like that, would you, Graw? If the Master went poof, you'd probably go poof too, or turn into a fossil—ho, ho, ho! While I stood up here on top of the mountain, laughing my head off!

"And what do you think I'd do next, Graw? When you and the Master had gone poof? Well, first of all I'd knock the top clear off this mountain so I could stand up straight without banging my head. I'd knock it off and fling it down there into the valley right onto that little village you can see down there. That'd wake 'em up that something unusual was going to happen! They'd look up, and then they'd see *me*, with my head sticking out of the top of the snow. Oh, that reminds me. I'd dig Old Paintpots out of her hole in the ground and I'd make her scrape all those awful colors off the snow. I might even make her eat the lot, caterpillars, hot snow, sticky snow, and all! The sight of so much whiteness would be the finish of her, I wouldn't wonder, mad old hag that she is. Then I'd climb out. My shadow would go right down the mountainside and fall on that village. Wouldn't they just die of fright when they saw the size of me! Ho, ho, ho, Grawkins! How they'd shriek and run, and then down the mountain I'd come in a few big strides, and I'd scoop them all up, little ants that they are next to me, and then I'd—I'd—"

The happy, excited voice of the giant petered out. It was as if he'd run out of ideas. He paused for a few moments and then muttered, "Well. Don't know what I'd do with them really. I might just sort of . . . No, that'd be no fun. Ah, they're so small. No good for slaves, no good for playing with or keeping in cages. . . . What's the use of them? . . . I dunno . . ." The muttering died away, and after a short while there was a trembling thud as the ogre's head fell back against the wall of the cave, and then great thunderous snores began, which made all the mountain rumble.

14
ANOTHER POEM

DAKIN VENTURED TO PEEP out, and up. She really couldn't
see much except what looked like a mountain of the
coarse cloth, and leather, and far, far up, a vast area of
hair—a jungle of hair, from which the snores seemed to be
coming. The candle was a giant holder on the floor, not
far away from her. Well, Drackamag was asleep, but where
was Graw? She crept out and looked all around the cave,
as much as she could for Drackamag's huge body, and
then she saw him. He was still firmly imprisoned in the
ogre's enormous hand, which had fallen back on his knee.
Only the creature's head stuck out from among the tree-
like fingers. Dakin could see he was struggling to free
himself, but it was useless. He was caught.

"If I had an ax," thought Dakin, "I could chop his head

off." And then she thought about doing it and added aloud, "No, I couldn't, not really . . ."

It was no trouble at all to crawl under the heavy folds of Drackamag's clothes to get through to the entrance to the passage. His bulk was blocking most of it, but she got there by running along a sort of channel in his jacket and then dropping through a hole she found in it. The worst part was going along the passage itself. Very little candlelight could pass the sleeping giant, so it was pitch dark. She ran along as fast as she dared and soon came to a turning. As she rounded it, a blinding light hit her eyes—the evening sun reflected on the colored snow. She was out!

What was more, the effect of the troll's magic bead had worn off. She could see herself again. And, she reminded herself, be seen.

She sat down in the mouth of the cave to think.

Far below she could see her own village. Drackamag's dream plan for what he would do if the Master were to go poof in the Lithy Pool was fresh in her memory. How easily she could imagine the panic and terror the ogre could cause if he ever showed himself on that side of the mountain! Far away it might be, but the ogre was big enough to frighten the life out of all her friends and neighbors if he ever did come bounding down the slope, crashing through the trees of the Wicked Wood, taking the fields and the river in one great stride, and then . . . Dakin shuddered. No, no—something had to be done. Something *had* to be done.

But what?

Dakin bit her lips and screwed her eyes shut. "Think, girl, think! Everything depends upon one thing: Who is the Master?" She had thought all along that Drackamag was. Graw was his watchdog: He was certainly the biggest thing alive on the mountain (or rather, in it) and all the decent creatures, the gargoyles and Croak and the troll, were afraid of him. But there was something—or some-body—worse than poor, brutal, stupid Drackamag. He'd talked as if the Master had *made* him. *And* brought Graw to life. Nothing could be done, Dakin decided, until she'd discovered who this Master was.

An idea came to her. Her book of poems had helped her before. Maybe it could again. She took it out of her pocket and let it fall open.

> Evil can come in many a guise,
> And wrong advice confuse the wise.
> Three good heads are better than one,
> Even though they be of stone.

Almost before she'd finished reading, Dakin was on her feet and peering all around her. The sun was just about to start sinking below the horizon. She had much less than an hour before nightfall. She must work quickly.

She was looking for the white trail she had kicked up in the morning coming up from the back entrance to the gargoyles' tunnel. If Zog was right, and the Colored Snow

Witch slept all day in what Drackamag had called her "hole in the ground," she wouldn't have had a chance to splash her magic colors around over the kicked-up white snow. Yes! There it was! And—oh, heavens! She'd almost forgotten, she was so used to going barefoot, that Graw had picked her up right out of her boots, which were still there, stuck to the yellow sticky snow. The short white trail below them must lead straight to the entrance to the tunnel, although she couldn't see it from here.

"Oh dear, oh dear!" thought Dakin in dismay. "How can I wade, or kick, or anything my way through this awful snow? Each color does a different kind of harmful magic. I managed it with boots to protect my feet, but now . . . !"

The snow at the edge of the castle cave door happened to be purple. It was a particularly horrid sort of purple, really poisonous-looking, and it seemed to be giving off a poisonous sort of smell. Dakin bent and sniffed at it from a safe distance. Oh yes—disgusting, and, how strange, just like the smell of Graw's wing. The thought of stepping on it with bare feet gave Dakin the shivers. But what could she do? Every moment was precious. The sun's lower rim was already touching the far-off horizon.

"This is the test, then," she thought, stiffening herself. "I must trust the Lithy Pool water. After all, Drackamag said it was so powerfully good that *he* had to build the cabin so he wouldn't have to look at it."

She lifted her long, full skirts, took a deep breath, and stepped into the purple snow.

It actually fizzled as her foot sank into it, and a cloud of evil-smelling purple steam rose up around her legs. Her feet felt very peculiar—quite numb—but she certainly didn't feel any pain or anything else, and after the first few steps she gained courage and walked boldly through: past the purple patch, into a navy blue patch (where all the snow melted away the second her foot touched it), through a green patch (the caterpillars formed under her feet, but scattered like slush under them as she walked), and a red patch (her feet smoked, but were not burned), to the yellow. Here she could feel that the sticky snow was trying to get a grip on her feet, but failing.

And now she'd reached her boots.

It was lovely to slip her cold feet into them. She took time to undo the laces and lace them up again tighter. Then she slipped down into the tunnel.

15
WHO IS THE MASTER?

SHE HAD NO CANDLE this time and it was much harder climbing down than it had been climbing up. She slid most of the way, and felt sure she would have been very badly grazed and bruised several times if it hadn't been for the magic of the water. The way was frightening and hard, but at last she was sticking her head out of the mouth of the cave on the other side of the mountain, where only this morning Drackamag had poked his finger, feeling for her.

"Zog!" she whispered loudly.

She saw a slight movement close by on the rock, and there was Zog's little face, all the carved lines upturned with joy at seeing her.

"AAAAAAAAAH!" he moaned with pleasure. "You're back! You're still alive! Oh, tell me, tell me—No, wait!"

He turned his head the other way on his long neck and made a strange gurgling whistle. Then he said, "I'm calling my brothers. You had better tell us all at once."

"But is it safe for them to leave their places?"

"Nothing is safe! But at evening Drackamag sleeps early, and sometimes when we are very lonely we meet together and talk."

Very soon first Vog, and then Og, came sliding around the corner of the rock face, and soon the three of them, like so many disembodied gnomes, were close to her, rubbing their hard, cold little heads against her and moaning "Aaaaaah!" until she put her hands to their mouths in turn to silence them.

"Shhhh!" she said. "Drackamag's asleep, but you never know who else might be watching or listening. . . ."

The gargoyles looked alarmed, and their necks twisted this way and that as they peered around.

"Who, who, who?" they asked, one after the other.

Dakin sat down on the ledge, and the brothers glided down to stay near her. Og and Zog rested their necks on her shoulders, and Vog, with a jealous look, nestled his head in her lap. Dakin petted him like a cat.

"Now, listen, all of you," she said, using the very firm tone of her mother when she had something serious and rather stern to say. "I see that we four are friends, and we are enemies of whatever the evil is that rules this mountain. No, now don't start 'ahhh-ing' straightaway; we've got to be very serious and we've all got to think."

The gargoyles all nodded their heads solemnly, and she went on:

"Now, you told me several things that I've been thinking about. First of all, you, Zog, said that you gargoyles are only sentinels and that you know nothing."

"True, true!" moaned Zog sadly.

"It is *not* true," said Dakin severely. "To begin with, you all know the password."

The gargoyles looked at each other.

"For another thing," Dakin went on, "you know what it is that the troll stole. Now, don't start fussing about what a deep secret *that* is, because I know already that he stole the Ring of Kings. But why couldn't you have told me that?" They all hung their heads. "But the most important thing of all is that I believe you know who the Master really is."

At this the gargoyles snatched themselves away from her and huddled all together, their necks entwined, their stone heads shivering so much that they grated together.

She parted them firmly with her hands.

"Enough of that," she said. "You'll chip each other's ears off. Now. Do you want the evil spell taken off this mountain or don't you?"

"We do, we do!" moaned the brothers.

"Then you'll have to help me, even if it *is* forbidden, even if it *is* dangerous. I've taken risks, and you'll have to take some too."

Again they looked at each other, and this time they slowly nodded.

"All right," said Dakin. "Now, first of all . . . the password."

Og slid up close to her and whispered, "Dragon's fin!"

"Oh, goodness! Is it still that? I knew that all the time. The troll said it would have been changed."

"She—he—never changes it," whispered Og.

"She? He? Who? The witch?"

The gargoyles were huddling again. Og looked miserable with terror.

"Yes—yes. The witch. Shhh! It's nearly dark. He—she—the witch will be waking up soon."

"But why are you all so afraid of her—I suppose the witch is a her?"

They didn't answer. The light was fading quickly now. Dakin shivered herself.

"Croak told me she was harmless, except for the magic colors she puts on the snow."

Again they were silent. Dakin suddenly felt very frightened. Could Old Croak have been wrong? She remembered the poem:

> *Evil can come in many a guise,*
> *And wrong advice confuse the wise . . .*

"How many years has Croak been shut in that cabin?" Dakin asked.

"Two hundred!" they moaned. "He has forgotten! He

knows only what Drackamag tells him. He doesn't even know who he once was, they say. . . ."

"That's true!" cried Dakin.

"Shhh!" the gargoyles hissed.

"But the witch—the witch can't be the Master! Drackamag isn't afraid of her! He said he'd dig her out and make her eat all her snow; he called her 'Old Paintpots.' "

Zog put his face to her ear and whispered, "*Drackamag himself* does not know the truth! The witch is only a disguise. The Master is the witch only at night. By day we do not know what he is, or where he is . . . that is the terrible thing! He is invisible. But his power—his voice—can be anywhere on the mountain. He may be here now!"

The four of them clung together, terrified. It was quite dark now, and the darkness seemed to press in upon them.

Dakin, suddenly loving them more than ever, pulled them to her and cuddled their cold heads.

"Did the witch change you, too? You weren't always like this?"

"Gargoyles everywhere were once people, or gnomes or trolls like us," explained Og. "We are lucky, in a way. We are still alive, we can still talk and think and move a little."

"We can still feel," said Vog, and they all nestled closer to her and moaned, "Ahhhhhh . . ." very softly.

"Why? Why didn't you become like other gargoyles, just stone heads?"

"The Master needed us to guard the mountain. He put us against the wall by the path. We are not allowed to meet together like this, and talk. If he ever caught us . . ."

"Ooooooooooh . . ."

"We would be broken off and thrown down the cliff or turned into ordinary gargoyles, unmoving, ugly, dead, forever!"

Dakin gently pushed them away and stood up.

"In that case," she said, "you must go back to your proper places. But before you go, is there *anything* else you can tell me that might be useful to me?"

From the darkness she heard three voices, one after the other:

"You cannot harm the Master by day. He is everywhere and nowhere. He is an evil spirit. He cannot be touched."

"At night he becomes the witch. He—she—seeks the ring by the light of the witch ball. Then he is visible, he has a body, he cannot melt into air until morning."

"The password will not protect you if he knows that you have come to save us. You must pretend you come with news of the ring. Then he will not harm you till he has it."

"But you said my troll stole the ring."

"Your troll, as you call him, is Gog, our fourth brother. He stole the ring at the christening of Prince Rally. He stole it because, like us, he was in the Master's power. He, too, was a flesh-and-blood troll then. We all went to the christening on the Master's orders. He told us that whoever stole the royal ring for him would be set free. Gog managed to slip it from the queen's finger as she was cuddling the baby and we were all pressing around to look. We four brothers ran with it back up the mountain.

"But on the way we began to quarrel. We knew that

when we returned to the Master, he would imprison us three again and let Gog go. It had been so lovely, that day of freedom! We couldn't bear the thought of being heads of stone again, perhaps for another hundred years. So we quarreled with God and he ran away from us, and that is the last we ever saw of him. But we know that the Master punished him from afar, for he knew what had happened, and although he has no power except on the mountain, he sent a spell which turned Gog into a small brass figure, just as Gog came to the far side of the Wicked Wood."

"That's where we found him!" exclaimed Dakin.

"And us he punished as you see. And ever since then, for seventeen years, he has been searching the woods by night, looking for the little brass troll who was our brother Gog."

"Oh! I do hope he got out of the wood all right," thought Dakin, and then she asked aloud, "Why did the Master—the witch—want the ring? Why is it so important?"

"First because it is magic. With that ring, he could take power over the whole country, not only this mountain."

"Also," said Vog, "without the ring, the prince cannot marry. It is the law of the land that that ring must be put on the finger of every royal bride. The royal family will die out without the ring, and since they are good and strong and take care of the people, the Master hates them."

"Now I understand," said Dakin. "Thank you. You've been very brave. Now go back to your places. I'm going to look for the witch."

16
THE WITCH

SHE KISSED EACH OF them and then climbed back into the cave. It was absolutely pitch black in there, and she popped straight out again.

"Are you still there?"

"We are just going."

"Blow on me before you go."

At once she felt rather than saw them cluster about her, and the next moment she felt their life-giving, strengthening breath envelop her. She tingled all over.

"Oh, that feels better! Thank you, dears. Now hurry, I'll be all right."

Back into the inky cave she crawled, and this time she hardly missed her eyes. Her hands and feet found holds by themselves, and as she moved along the tunnel, her mind was working quickly.

"Only at night is the Master solid and only at night can he be harmed. But at night he takes the shape of a witch. Now, what did Old Croak say? That there's only one thing the witch is afraid of, and that's the color white. But Old Croak was wrong about a lot of things. How wise am I to rely on *that*? On the other hand, what else can I rely on?

"Now, what have I got that's white? My apron . . . that's quite big. The only trouble is it's filthy; it's really not white any longer. My petticoats! Let me think, did I put a white one on, or are they all red flannel?" She stopped, picked up the edge of her skirt, and fumbled among the petticoats. Flannel. Flannel. Flannel. "Oh, dear, oh dear!" she said aloud. "It's my own fault for being too lazy to iron a cotton one!"

Suddenly a sharp voice said, "Password."

Dakin froze. The evil smell she'd noticed before was all about her. She saw a round, greenish light, and a strange figure behind it.

"Dragon's fin!"

"Too late for that," said the voice.

"Who are you?"

"I am the artist whose painting you destroyed with your clumsy feet," said the voice softly.

"You are also the Master of the mountain," Dakin said, and wondered what had made her say anything so dangerous.

There was a silence, and then the voice, sounding somehow much more menacing than before, said: "Those who have betrayed me shall be punished. And you shall see it done."

The horror of the ogre's nail feeling for her in the cave, the horror of Graw's wing brushing her face, the horror of the slimy caterpillers and all the other signs of evil at work: none had turned her blood to ice as that voice did; and how much more terrifying it was when, without warning, she felt a cold, clammy hand suddenly clutch her wrist and begin dragging her along, back the way she had just come.

With her free hand she pulled and scratched at the thing that held her, but it was like tearing at an iron band. Willy-nilly she was pulled along, stumbling over the rocks, and finally she could see the cave mouth with the starlight twinkling in it.

"Oh, Og! Oh, Vog! Oh, Zog!" was all she could think through her terror, for the feeling of the Lithy Water was still strong, protecting *her*—but what about *them*? How could she save them?

For a moment something black blocked the mouth of the cave as the witch scrambled through, then Dakin was pulled through after her. The next thing she knew was that she was standing out on the ledge.

A full moon was rising over the valley, bathing everything in a cold, eerie light. A *white* light. The witch, a withered-looking crone dressed in rags of many colors, all bleached and unnatural in the moonlight, immediately shrank from the white moon and made a flickering, jerky movement in front of her eyes with her free hand. At once, to Dakin's astonishment—it seemed so very odd—a pair of dark glasses, just like the ones the blind man in her village wore, appeared on the witch's nose. From her arm hung the silver witch ball that gave off a cold green light. It shone upon the most terrible face Dakin had ever seen or dreamed of.

Dakin thought she heard a faint, frightened hiss behind her. Stealthily groping with her free hand, she felt Zog huddling against the cliff face. She dared to cuddle him, and in turn she felt him breathing on her hand with all his might. A great wave of strength went up her arm.

"Now, meddlesome girl," said the witch, "we will talk. But first . . ." With a sudden jerk, Dakin was pulled away from the cliff, leaving Zog exposed. He curled his neck and tried to hide his face, but the witch pointed her bony finger at him.

"You," she said in a voice so full of menace that Drackamag's loudest roar seemed like the purr of a kitten beside it. "Go and fetch your brothers. Do not try to escape, for my power is upon you all! Enjoy the little moments of life and the freedom to move and speak that are still left to you. Go."

With a whimper of terror, and one piteous look at Dakin, poor Zog slipped away around the corner.

"What are you going to do to them?" cried Dakin.

"You shall see it all," said the witch in a cruel, singsong

voice. "You shall see how, with the edge of my hand, I can strike them from their roots in the rock and send them tumbling down the cliff to smash into a thousand lifeless pieces of stone at the bottom!"

"Oh no! Oh no!"

"They have lived too long. They are only slaves, and they have disobeyed my orders. I shall send them to their deaths, as I have already sent their brother Gog."

As she said these words, the witch jerked Dakin sharply toward her by the wrist and peered closely into her face. The smell of evil nearly made Dakin sick.

"Have you nothing to say?" the witch hissed.

The last thing Dakin wanted to do was to tell this dreadful, wicked creature the truth about Gog, her troll. Yet something in the eyes that seemed to flicker through the dark glasses forced her to speak when she had not meant to.

"Gog isn't dead," she gasped.

"Ah!"

The clutch on Dakin's wrist tightened.

"But he is outside your power. He is off the mountain!" Dakin added.

"I knew it!" said the witch. "Signs and portents! Signs and portents! I have my ways! And he is down there in the valley, and my ring with him!"

"He has no ring!" said Dakin. "He is only small. . . . I can hold him in my hand! I could have seen if he had a ring anywhere about him."

She stopped, her free hand to her mouth. She was

remembering how her troll had looked as he had stood on her hand in the Wicked Wood. And suddenly she *saw* the ring—she knew where it was!

Clearly it came back to her: Gog, her little brass troll, standing on her palm, with a thick gold belt around his

tiny waist, *a smooth belt with no buckle*. She had thought it brass, like him, but now she knew it was the very Ring of Kings that he had stolen. It had become a part of him when the spell, flung down the mountain after him by the Master, had changed him into a brass figure.

17
THE STORY OF
THE MOUNTAIN

IT WAS A TERRIBLE moment, because she knew now that the witch had power to force her to speak the truth against her will. The witch must have seen Dakin's change of expression when she realized where the ring was. In another second she would make her say what her thought had been.

Dakin had to do something instantly.

Her free right hand, still tingling from Zog's breath, acted by itself. Her fingers hooked themselves around the tops of the witch's glasses, pulled them off, and flung them down the cliff.

As the witch turned to try to grab them, she was faced with the moon, now clear of the horizon and shining, huge and white, toward them. With a scream, the witch let go of Dakin and covered her eyes with both hands. When her hands came down a second later, another pair of dark glasses was on her nose, and the next thing Dakin knew was that she had been pulled off her feet and was hanging by her hands off the edge of the ledge, her feet dangling clear over a thousand-foot drop.

The witch, still on the ledge, bent down and peered, laughing, into her terrified face.

"Now you are no danger to me," she said. "I should have thought of that before. We can talk like this, and when we have finished talking, if I find I have no more use for you, I can just—"

A long, black foot appeared, just over one of Dakin's hands, which was clutching the ledge.

Then the witch sat down, arranging her wild-colored tatters around her as if making herself very comfortable.

"Do you like stories?" she asked. "I will tell you one. Many years ago there was, among all the old, dead mountains in this land, one mountain different from all the others. This mountain was not dead. It had a soul. In the old days, you may know, men believed that many things had souls— trees, wells, fields, lakes. . . . Nowadays no one believes this, and it is, in general, no longer true. But this one mountain had kept its soul within it from those past times.

"Because of its soul, the mountain had strange powers. Men who tried to come near it found it always got farther and farther away, so none could reach it, except a few whom the soul of the mountain called. Because the soul was a *good* soul"—and here the witch shuddered—"it called only to those who were very good among men, or trolls; and those it called would come, and live on its slopes, and create gardens, and plant forests. They were few, but they were very happy." The witch shuddered again.

"But then," she went on, chuckling a little, "something went wrong. Some two hundred years ago, the mountain nodded to a young man who then lived in the very same village where you dwell. This young man was something extraordinary even among the good people of the world. He was a scholar, gentle, kind, learned, and generous." After each of these words, the witch grimaced as if saying them gave her pain. "But he was not wise. He had among his pupils a boy, the son of a black magician, who was as filled with wickedness as his teacher was filled with goodness. When the young man, whose name was Ravik, received his call from the mountain, he was full of joy, for he knew he was going to a place like heaven on earth; and he decided to take with him this boy, in order to rid the village of his dangerous magic, and believing that the good influence of the mountain would change his wicked ways.

"So he led him up to the mountain. The boy walked behind him, and as he walked, the green of the slopes withered to blackness where he trod, the trees died, and the birds fell out of them, the sun grew dark, and all life fled away. All the good people of the mountain gathered together. They saw this Evil One approaching and cried out to young Ravik, 'What are you bringing upon us? Take it away! Take it away!' for the boy could not disguise his true nature from their eyes. But Ravik said, 'Enough good will outweigh evil. Among so many who are good his wickedness will get lost, and he will be cured.' But they ran from him and left him alone with his pupil.

"Now, this mountain was magic, and its magic was strong upon all those people. Yet for all their goodness, they had too little courage, and when they ran away they left an emptiness which the Evil Boy filled. As the young man Ravik turned to him in dismay and saw for the first time the trail of death and destruction his passing had left, the boy seemed to grow and grow before his eyes, looming above him; and Ravik fell backward, covering his eyes. And when he opened them again, he was a little, helpless frog."

"Oh, my poor Croak!" thought Dakin, holding on with all her might.

"After that, the Evil Boy took over the mountain. Its soul could not be destroyed, but was put to sleep, deep in the heart of the rock. The Evil One summoned slaves and created a monster to do his bidding. He brought back to life a creature long passed from the world, to guard it and do his will. He made the mountain the home of evil. He tried to extend his powers, but this he could not do without the help of a magic ring owned by the kings of the world of men below. Once, it was almost within his grasp, but a worthless slave of a troll fled from his Master and escaped somehow. . . ." The witch gnashed her teeth and howled with fury, remembering this. . . . "And now the Evil One, as punishment for this one piece of carelessness, must give all his time to searching and searching for this ring, that he may spread his reign over all the world of men, destroying what is good and increasing what is bad until the whole world is like this mountain—a black fountain of evil, pouring over all!"

Horrified and frightened as she was, Dakin refused to let her fear overpower her. The lesson of the story was clear. It wasn't enough to be good, one had to be wise and brave as well. The young man Ravik had been good, but not wise, and so he had brought evil into the magic mountain. The people of the mountain had been good, but not brave: They had run away and left the mountain in the power of the Evil Boy, who now, two hundred years later, was both the Master and the Witch.

Whether she herself was good or not, Dakin did not stop to think. What mattered now was to be wise and brave. The witch must be destroyed before morning came and she vanished again. She must be destroyed even sooner, before the gargoyles returned to meet their awful punishment.

18
THE WITCH BALL

HER HANDS AND ARMS, even with the magic of Zog's breath to strengthen them, were beginning to ache dreadfully. She doubted very much if even the Lithy Pool water could save her life if she fell. How long could she hang on here? And if she made any move, would the witch now carry out her threat to tread on her fingers and make her let go?

Dakin knew there was only one hope. It was terribly dangerous.

"I'm going to fall!" she cried out suddenly.

"Fall then," said the witch coldly. "It will please me to watch it."

"But you forget, Master of the Mountain!" cried Dakin. "You forget the ring!"

"Ah!" hissed the witch. "Then you know where it is?"

"Of course I know. Get me up and I'll tell you."

"Tell me first!"

"No. Pull me up, and I'll not only tell you where the ring is, I'll get it for you."

The witch hesitated. Then she took hold of Dakin's wrists in her clammy hands and lifted her back onto the ledge. Then, to Dakin's astonishment, she let her go.

"Stand still," she hissed. "Look!"

She lifted the witch ball by its string, which hung from her arm, and slowly passed it to and fro in front of Dakin's eyes.

"Look into my witch ball!" she said.

But Dakin did not look. Another voice—a voice she had heard only once before—spoke inside her head.

"Do not look at it," said this voice. "If you do, you will become helpless. Look into the witch's eyes."

Dakin gasped. The voice was the same she had heard in her sleep, the morning the mountain had called her.

With all the strength of her will, she kept her eyes away from the glowing greenish ball swinging back and forth before her face. She fixed them instead upon the two dark circles through which the witch's eyes glittered.

"Are you looking at the ball?" asked the witch in a low monotonous voice.

"Yes," said Dakin.

"Then tell me the truth about the ring."

"Do you know how to answer?" asked the voice in Dakin's head.

And, strangely, Dakin did.

"It is in the Lithy Pool," said Dakin clearly.

The witch gave a long, drawn-out hiss and seemed to shrink into her colored tatters. She let the witch ball fall from her fingers. It was still swinging to and fro, and the sudden jerk as it dropped to the end of its string made it fly against the cliff wall.

It shattered. But the sound was not just the clash of thin glass. It was an explosion, with a blinding green flash and a puff of evil-smelling green smoke. The witch reeled back and would have fallen if she had not clutched at Dakin.

"My witch ball! My witch ball!" she shrieked. Then she turned to Dakin in wild fury. "See what you've done! You'll pay for this! You'll pay!"

"Yes, I'll pay," said Dakin quickly. "I'll pay by getting you the ring."

19
DOOM

THE WITCH STARED AT her, her breath coming in gasping wheezes. She no longer looked sure of herself, and Dakin guessed that part of her power had left her when the witch ball had smashed.

"Yes. The ring," she whispered at last. "Quickly. We must get it quickly, before day comes. Come here!"

With a quick, jerky movement, the witch pulled Dakin up against her and threw her ragged cloak around her until she was completely covered by it. Almost overpowered by being so close to the source of evil, Dakin nearly fainted and did not know what happened next; but it seemed only a few seconds later that the smelly cloak was whisked off again and she found herself standing in Croak's cabin.

It was very dark in there (the moon was on the other side of the mountain), but a trace of reflected starlight came through the windows and glittered faintly on the surface of the Lithy Pool.

The witch seemed oddly nervous and agitated.

"Now," she hissed. "Be quick!"

"You'll have to give me some light," said Dakin, thinking furiously.

The witch made some sharp, jerky passes in the air with her hands. A very faint light appeared in the cabin, and Dakin immediately gave a quick look around for Croak, but couldn't see him—he was probably hiding. Almost at once, the light faded again. She heard the witch muttering curses and saw her moving her hands as before, only more frantically. And suddenly Dakin realized what was wrong with her. The nearness of the Lithy Pool was sapping what little power she still had; to stand beside it like this, without her witch ball to protect her, was exhausting her.

The faint green light appeared again, weaker than before.

"There!" said the witch, and now she seemed to be gasping for breath. "Go in and get it! If you cannot, nothing will save you—nothing!"

"I must have more light," said Dakin, for now an idea was forming in her mind. "I need enough light to shine down through the water."

"The pool has no bottom," hissed the witch. "That is known."

"Nonsense," said Dakin, trusting that the witch's natural

115

fear of the pool would have prevented her checking for herself how deep it was. "It's quite shallow. By day I could see the ring twinkling on the bottom."

"What? How did it get there?"

"I threw it in myself, yesterday," said Dakin carelessly.

The witch gave a snarl of rage. But she could do nothing except exert every effort to brighten the light. She muttered a spell, and worked and labored over it until her whole crooked body seemed to be jerking and writhing. At

last she succeeded. A series of bright green flashes lit up the cabin, throwing the witch's angular, twisting shadow onto the walls.

"Hurry! Hurry!" shrieked the witch.

Dakin did hurry. She dared not stop to think about the danger. With one hand she reached for the witch's dark glasses, snatched them off as before, and threw them into the pool. At the same moment, with the other, she pulled off her white stocking cap and waved it in front of the witch's face.

The witch screamed and hid her eyes.

Dakin knew from the last time that in a matter of a second the witch would have made another pair of glasses to protect her from the dreaded whiteness. But in that one instant, Dakin got behind her and pushed with all her might.

The witch tottered for a moment on the brink of the pool and then, with a horrible shriek, fell in.

There was no splash. The waters opened to receive her and closed over her again. Dakin's feet were soaked by the wave that came out all around the edge. In the last of the magic light, Dakin saw what Drackamag had meant. The witch—the Evil Master—did indeed go "poof." In eerie silence, a cloud of green smoke puffed out of a little whirlpool, which was all that was left to show where she had gone. Then the water settled down to glassy calm again in the peaceful starlight.

20
TROLLS

SUDDENLY EVERYTHING WAS DIFFERENT.

It was impossible to say how, but it was as if some great weight had been lifted off everything. Dakin picked herself up and looked around. The smoke was thinning and blowing away in the breeze. The stench was still there, but growing less every moment. The air seemed to beat like a pulse. Dakin felt overwhelmed with some feeling that might be called happiness for lack of some stronger word. She simply stood there, breathing lightly, enjoying this feeling in every part of her.

Something touched her knee.

She looked down. A little man stood there, and another, and a third. Their faces in the moonlight looked familiar.

"It is me, Og," said the first in a voice of wonder and joy. "And look! I am free!"

"And I!"

"And I! We are all trolls again—ourselves, as we used to be. Oh, what did you do? We thought we were to die, and instead we are restored!"

Dakin crouched down, and the three brothers, sad, imprisoned gargoyles no more but flesh-and-blood little men, stood close to her, looking shyly and marvelingly into her face. She touched each one gently, and each one in turn blushed deeply and murmured, "Ahhh. . . ."

"My little friends!" she said softly. "I'm so glad!"

And suddenly they all flung themselves on her and hugged and kissed her.

"But how? What? How?" they all asked breathlessly, and Vog added, "We were coming back, very, very slowly, thinking we were living our last moments, when suddenly there was a loud noise, and the next minute . . . we were standing here."

Dakin told them all that had happened.

They stared at her.

"How brave," murmured Zog.

"Oh, nonsense," said Dakin. "I simply had to. And after that strange voice spoke inside my head, it wasn't so difficult."

"But that voice must have been the voice of your own thoughts," said Og.

"No! Not at all. It was nothing to do with me. I'm sure of that."

"You say it was the same voice that called you to come to the mountain?" said Vog slowly.

"Yes, I'm sure it was the same. I heard it in my sleep."

"And afterward you saw the mountain nod?"

"Yes."

The three brothers looked at each other.

"I wonder . . ." said Og.

"It couldn't be," said Vog.

"Are you certain of that?" said Zog.

"What are you talking about?" asked Dakin.

But they wouldn't tell her.

"I wish our brother Gog were here," said Zog.

Suddenly Vog jumped up. "Gog will be like us! The spell is broken; he will be a live troll again!" he cried.

"What will he do?" asked Dakin.

"Surely he will come back? This mountain was our home in the good days before the Evil One came."

"Well, he's got a long way to come," said Dakin. "Meantime, I wish you'd tell me what you were talking about before—about the voice."

"We are probably wrong," said Zog. Then he pointed through the window. "Look, the moon is setting! It will soon be morning. Let's sleep. Oh, how lovely it will be to sleep again! We haven't slept for two hundred years."

The trolls lay down in the cabin then and there, yawning and stretching, and in a moment they were all snoring blissfully.

Now Dakin had time to look for Old Croak.

All through the rest of the night, she called and searched for him. She turned over every leaf, groped into every shadow. She even lay down by the pond and reached her arms in as far as they would go, stirring the water and calling all the time:

"Croak! Croak! Where are you?"

Nothing.

The dawn crept across the meadow, the first bird notes sounded, and in a few minutes, as if those firstawake birds had realized that all was changed, every living creature in meadow and wood seemed to burst into song. As the sun began to flood the mountain Dakin took a last look around. She still felt that powerful joy underlying her awful disappointment that Croak had vanished. Nevertheless, tears poured down her cheeks.

"Oh, Croak," she sobbed. "Don't be dead! I can't bear it if you're dead!"

Croak—or, rather, Ravik—had been turned into a frog two hundred years ago. When the witch's death broke the spell, Croak might have changed back into a man—a two-hundred-year-old man. He would die at once from old age.

But then, where was his body?

And if it worked like that, why weren't the brothers old? But trolls live longer than people and don't age in the same way.

At last Dakin got up. It was no use sitting there crying. She had to find Gog and get the Ring of Kings back to the palace. She wished she felt more excited about seeing the Prince, who, she felt sure, was destined to be her husband.

She had never seen him. But of course he must be tall and handsome and so on—who ever heard of a prince who wasn't? Nevertheless, she really felt, as she climbed up the chimney, that she'd rather have seen her dear Croak at that moment than the handsomest prince on earth.

21
CHANGES

As THE SUN ROSE clear of the peak, Dakin raised her eyes and nearly laughed with relief. All the snow was white! That much at least of the evil magic had died with its maker.

Suddenly her smile froze. Somebody was coming down the mountain.

It was a man, rather undersized but not a troll, wearing shabby green trousers and thick boots; he had an untidy, bushy beard and thick, uncut hair. On his rather stupid-looking face was a dazed expression, as if he'd only just wakened and couldn't remember where he was. In his hand was a dark gray parrot.

Of course, you will guess at once that this was all that was left of the terrible ogre and his pet. But Dakin, though she knew it too really, could not believe it at first. After seeing him in his gigantic state, and having been nearly frightened out of her wits by Graw, it took some time before she could realize that this perfectly harmless-looking fellow and the blinking, fluttering parrot were these same two monsters of only the day before.

She stood still in the meadow, and the man, seeing her, turned and came slowly up to her.

"Excuse me, miss," he said. "Do you know where we are?"

"We're on the farthest-away mountain," said Dakin faintly, staring at him.

"I dunno . . . It's all very queer," muttered the man. "I just woke up in some sort of huge cave up there. Pitch dark it was. And I had this here bird in my hand. It bit me. Frightened me half to death, it did. . . . Now it won't leave me. . . . Funny, I can't seem to remember how I got there. Where are you from?"

"That village in the valley," said Dakin, pointing downward.

"Village?" said the man. "That's right, I come from a village too. I remember now. I was out walking and I had a sudden fancy to explore this mountain. Just kept walking and walking, and . . ." He frowned and shook his head. "No, it's no use. I can't remember anything more. Funny . . . Maybe I'd had too much to drink. . . . There's something wrong with my eyes too. Everything looks big to me this morning. . . . Well, I think I'd best be walking back down again."

He nodded to her politely and set off downward toward the wood.

22
HOME

THE MEADOW HAD BEEN a happy place even in the time of
the Evil One, because of the good influence of the Lithy
Pool, Dakin supposed. But now it was like paradise. The
sun shone, and every part of the meadow seemed bursting
with life. Even the dark wood at the far end no longer
looked sinister, and when she reached it she found that
the branches overhead no longer entirely kept the sun's
rays out. It was quite bright in there, and lots of little
woodland creatures had already invaded it. The branches
were laden with birds, and small animals scurried here
and there almost under her feet as she hurried along, half
expecting to meet Gog at any moment.

She didn't meet him. Instead she walked on and on, following the direction of the pine needles as before, until, after about three hours, she suddenly felt very faint and sat down sharply.

"Whatever's the matter with me?" she thought. She put her head on the forest floor, but still everything spun, around and around. What was it?

"I'm hungry," she thought. "Of course I must be! I haven't eaten a thing for two days. Goodness, how silly if I were to die of hunger here in the wood after all that's happened! I feel so weak I can't go on. . . ."

The next thing she knew, she was being lifted and a man's voice was saying, "Poor child! She's fainted. How lucky we came this way to look for her. . . . No, I'll carry her myself. Her mother will be so happy to see her. . . ."

She opened her eyes a little, then closed them again. She was being tenderly carried in strong arms. She seemed to sleep. When she opened her eyes again, she was lying in the living room at home, and her mother, and father, and Triska, and Margle, and Sheggie, and Dawsy were all standing around her looking at her anxiously and solemnly.

"I'm fine," she said at once. "Don't look so worried."

Then they all seemed to change. Her mother burst into tears and so did Sheggie. Triska jumped up and down and squealed. Margle and Dawsy hugged each other and did a sort of men's dance around the room. And her father just kept shaking his head and blowing his nose.

"Where were you? Where were you?" they all kept asking.

But before Dakin could answer, another face appeared beside her, the kind, stern face of the village doctor.

"Now then, no tales just yet," he said. "She must rest, and drink her warm milk. Come along, my girl, get this inside you. The talking comes later."

So Dakin drank her milk, and Margle carried her up to bed, and she lay there for a while, looking out of the window at the farthest-away mountain. The snow looked pure white now. Just before she dropped off to sleep, she thought she heard the strange voice in her head, now bell-clear, say:

"Thank you, child. Sleep well. Your task is done."

23
THE RING

In the middle of the night she woke up.

She sat up sharply in bed and, with fumbling hands, lit the candle. She had been dreaming of the ring. There was something she had to know. Moving as quietly as she had the morning she set out, she tiptoed down the stairs in her bare feet and went into the kitchen. She held the candle high as she approached the mantelpiece. The little light caught a gleam of brass at one end.

It was Gog.

It was really Gog, but still small, still brass, and now— unmoving, a little lifeless figure as he had always been!

"Gog!" she whispered. "The spell's broken! Why aren't you a real troll again, like your brothers?"

He neither moved nor spoke. She touched his belt with

her fingers. Yes, there was no doubt about it. It was the Ring of Kings. It was loose—she could twist it around his waist. But it wouldn't come off.

How was this possible? In the wood, he had come to life and spoken to her. Then he had run away. Then what? He had come back here, jumped onto the mantelpiece, and—become a statue again? She shook him sharply.

"Gog!" she almost shouted.

"Dakin? Is that you?"

It was her mother's voice. In another minute her mother was beside her.

"Daughter, what are you doing out of bed? Come, child, you're not well yet. Let me take you back upstairs."

"Mother! Our troll . . . Was he missing?"

Her mother stared at her.

"Why, yes," she said. "Triska noticed it, the morning you disappeared. And that same evening, she found him out in the garden. She went on and on about it, because she said he was quite different, that all the tarnish was gone, and that he was in a different position. She even said his face was different. I must say I was too upset to look closely. Though now I notice," she added, taking the figure out of Dakin's hand, "it is very odd, for as I remember he was seated before, and now he is standing up. Perhaps it is another one altogether?"

"No, Mother. It's the same one. I know by his belt."

"How strange! It is not part of him—see—it turns around. It would make a fine ring if one could get it off. One might

130

think it was gold. But one couldn't get it off except by cutting the figure in half, and you wouldn't want—"

"No, no!"

"Come. Up to bed, and I'll sing you to sleep."

Dakin took Gog to bed with her and kept him warm all night in her hand. She half hoped to bring him to life that way, but when she woke in the morning he was just as before.

24
THE PALACE

DAKIN STAYED IN BED for several days until she was quite well and strong again. All the time she was thinking. She knew the next thing to do was to take the ring back to the palace, which was at the further end of the valley, in the middle of the royal estates. But one thing troubled her. How could the ring be got off? If there was no other way than by cutting Gog in half, the King and Queen would want to do that, and how could Dakin explain that that was quite out of the question?

At last she was well enough to get up. That day nobody in the family did any work. They all sat around Dakin and listened breathlessly while she told them her story. At first the older ones would not believe. But there had been a lot of talk in the village about strange differences in the mountain. The villager who had found Dakin in the forest said that something had almost seemed to pull him forward to where she was lying. Others said they were not afraid of the wood anymore, and many children had begun to cross the river (which had always been forbidden) and play under the trees. None had got lost or come to any harm. Everyone had noticed that the snow no longer changed color.

The pastor was sent for, to hear Dakin's story. He listened very gravely and then went away to look up the old books, kept locked in a cupboard in the church, in which were written the names of all the people who had ever been born in the village and what had happened to them; these were called the pastoral records. He returned with one of the books, surely the oldest book Dakin had ever seen. He opened it at one yellow page and pointed to a name written in ink that had faded to pale brown with age.

The name was Ravik.

The record said he had been born two hundred and twenty-two years ago, and that at the age of twenty-two he had walked up the mountain and never been seen again. The record of the Evil Boy and his father, the black magician, was there, too. The pastor would not let Dakin read about the things they had done, but he showed it to Dakin's father, and they shook their heads and looked very grim. The boy had disappeared on the same day as Ravik.

So then they all believed her.

Margle spoke for them all when he said, "Our Dakin is a heroine."

They treated her like a queen for several days until Dakin thought she would scream if it went on any longer. So she did a number of naughty things on purpose until her mother lost patience and gave her a smack on the bottom, and after that everyone forgot she was a heroine and re-membered that, after all, she was only their own Dakin, and began to treat her normally. After that she was much happier.

But the matter of the ring was not settled, and at last her father said:

"Dakin, the royal family must be told we have the ring. Come, I will take you there. We'll explain everything to the King. He is a good man, and won't do anything to your troll."

Dakin was not so sure, but indeed word had reached them that the royal family was getting more and more up-set about the missing ring as Prince Rally drew near to his eighteenth birthday, which is the age when, by tradition, the princes of that land got married. A huge reward had been offered to anyone who found it, and though Dakin didn't care about the reward, she was nearly fifteen herself and knew that if she were going to marry her prince there was no use putting it off.

So her mother dressed her in her very best and brushed her hair till it glistened, and she and her father drove down the valley to the royal estate in a pony trap.

It was a glorious summer's day. The valley was blooming; all the farmers went out in their fields and the women were finding excuses to work outdoors, too. As they drove past, Dakin waved to friends and strangers alike, thinking gaily, "If only they knew that soon I shall be a princess!" Now the time was so near, though her sadness about Croak did keep coming back to her every now and then.

Gog was in the pocket of her best apron. She kept touching him as if to reassure him. "I won't let them do anything to you," she whispered as they reached the palace and, giving the pony to one of the royal grooms, walked boldly up to the great gates and knocked.

A uniformed guard opened a small door in the gate.

"We've come to see His Majesty," said Dakin's father.

"What is your business?" asked the guard haughtily.

"We have found the ring" was the answer.

That changed everything, and very quickly too. The guard turned pale. He stepped back and gave a signal. At once the great gates swung open and an armed guard of six soldiers stepped forward to escort them to the King.

Now Dakin really did feel excited. Up the long flights of steps they marched, with the guards' bright silver breastplates and helmets gleaming and their white plumes nodding, and when they reached the end of a long carpeted corridor, the first guard had a word with two other soldiers, who immediately raised trumpets to their lips and blew a fine, tuneful blast on them which said without words:

"Here comes someone of the greatest importance to see Their Majesties!"

Then double doors swung open and they were in a great long chamber with two thrones on a dais at the end of it and a red carpet leading to them. Seated on the thrones were the King and Queen.

"Who is this?" asked the King.

Dakin's father turned to one of the guards. "Tell him we have the ring," he said, in a modest way.

But the chamber had an echo, and the King heard what he'd said and leaped to his feet.

"The ring! Did you say you have the *ring*?" he cried in the greatest excitement. "My dear, they have it! These people have the ring!" he added, turning to the Queen, who also jumped up, and to Dakin's delight they actually hugged each other.

"Come, come quickly!" the King called down the room to them, so they hurried along the red carpet, with the six guards almost running to keep up, and the King came down the steps to the dais to meet them and wrung their hands so hard it hurt, and at the same time said, "Where is it, where is it?" and held out his hand for it eagerly.

25
RALLY

"Give His Majesty the ring, Dakin," said her father. But Dakin kept her hand in her pocket.

"I'll show it to you," she said. "I'm afraid I can't give it to you, because—well, it's rather a long story." And she told it to them as briefly as she could and then, while they were still gaping at her in amazement, held out the little brass troll and showed them the ring.

The King peered at it closely, and so did the Queen.

"It's the Ring of Kings all right," said the King. "It has come back to us. What a relief! I see the problem, of course. It is a hard one to solve. But surely some answer will be found. We must not let a little difficulty stand in the way of a celebration. Come, my dear," he added to the Queen. "We must introduce this young lady to Rally. He is free to marry now, and I'm sure he'll wish to thank her personally."

"To thank me?" thought Dakin. "To marry me, you mean!" But of course she did not say so aloud. "When he sees me," she thought, "he will know at once that I am meant for him."

Meanwhile the Queen had clapped her hands and a servant had appeared.

"Send for the Prince," she said.

"And bring some chairs, so that we may all be comfortable," added the King.

Some big, richly upholstered chairs, almost more like thrones, were quickly brought, and the royal couple graciously asked Dakin and her father to be seated. The grown-ups talked, but Dakin was watching the little door through which the servant had gone. After a while she heard footsteps coming. She straightened herself, smoothed her apron, and pushed a curl of hair behind her ear, her heart beating hard. He was coming—her prince!

The door opened, and in walked the most dreary-looking young man Dakin had ever seen.

Her mouth fell open. No. It just couldn't be. Not that little, skinny, miserable youth with the skimpy beard and the stooped shoulders and the weak chin! *This* couldn't be he! Why, she wouldn't marry *him* if he were the last young man in the world!

"Ah, Rally," said the Queen, "come over here and meet the girl who has found our ring."

The young man shuffled over and threw her a look out of his pale, disinterested eyes.

"Oh?" he said. "Quite clever of her, eh? Where was it?"

"That's a long story, my boy," said the King heartily. "She'll tell it to you, no doubt, if you ask her politely."

"Oh, I don't think I'll bother," said the Prince. "So long as it's back, that's all that matters. I suppose that means that now I can marry Zendrina. She's a boring creature, but never mind, we don't have to see much of each other, and I'll be able to concentrate on my butterfly collection instead of worrying about the ring the whole time."

There was a short silence, and then his mother said with a bright smile, "Well, Rally? Have you nothing more to say to the young lady?"

The Prince looked blank, and then said, "Have I? I don't know. . . . What? Do you want to look at my collection?" he asked Dakin. "I've got some fine specimens, you know, all pinned to pieces of wood. I'll show them to you if you like."

"No, thank you," said Dakin quickly.

The King tried to hide his irritation and gave the Prince a heavy pat on the back. It was more like a whack really, and Rally nearly fell on his face.

"*Thank* her, you young blockhead!" he said, pretending it was a joke.

"Oh—oh yes. Thanks and so forth," said Rally. He stifled a yawn.

Dakin suddenly bowed her head and her shoulders rose and fell.

Her father leaned down to her. "What is it, Dakin? Don't you feel well?"

She shook her head.

"Your Majesty, my daughter has been ill. May I take her out onto the balcony for some fresh air?"

"Of course! Of course!" said the King.

Dakin and her father crossed the room and went out onto a wide stone balcony overlooking the valley.

"What is it, darling? Why are you crying?"

"Oh, Father! Oh, Father!" was all Dakin could say between her sobs.

She was holding Gog in her hands, and as she cried, her tears fell on him. And suddenly, just as before, he sneezed and sat up.

26
GOG

SHE FELT HER FATHER clutch her shoulder and stagger backward in amazement. But she was so overjoyed she could hardly keep from jumping up and down.

"Gog! Gog!" she cried softly, so as not to attract the attention of the royal family.

"Thank heavens!" said Gog. "I thought you'd *never* have sense enough to cry on me again! Lend me your handkerchief."

"What happened, Gog? What happened?"

"It's all quite simple," said the troll, wiping the tears off his hat just like the last time. "Tears are magic, as no doubt you know by now. Not very powerful, but still magic. They give me a few hours of life—life of a sort, of

141

course. So after I—er—after we separated," he said with a cough (Dakin guessed he felt rather ashamed of having deserted her), "I ran home as fast as I could . . . to your home, I mean, of course. Just as I reached the garden gate, the magic wore off. It was very lucky your little sister found me, or I might have lain out there getting tarnished again. So. Now I suppose you want the ring. Oh, it's all right, I heard you tell the whole story. . . . Even when I'm not able to move or speak, I can still hear. Well, I suppose I've got no further use for it, and I'm not at all anxious to be chopped in half. That young man would do it without thinking twice about it, no doubt. Here." And he put both thumbs into the top of the ring and wriggled out of it as easily as taking off his trousers. He picked it up and handed it to Dakin.

"What were the tears about, anyway?" he asked her with a sharp look in his little brass eyes.

Dakin didn't answer.

"Disappointed, eh?" he asked. "Well, well. That's how it goes. Nobody ever gets exactly what he wants in this world. Magic or no magic. What makes you think you'd have liked being a princess, anyway?"

"Ah," said Dakin's father. "Now I understand! Poor girl . . ." But to Dakin's annoyance she saw he couldn't help laughing as he glanced over his shoulder at the weedy figure of Prince Rally in the throne room. "So that was what you had in mind, daughter? No, no, he's not for you! Better come home and marry young Ruston. He's still waiting. . . ." But Dakin tossed her head and turned her back on him.

While all this was going on on the balcony, the King had not been idle. He had called his heralds and ordered them to ride out all over the country to announce that the ring had been found and that there would be a great national celebration in a week's time for the Prince's wedding. Naturally Dakin and her whole family were invited to come to the palace for this, as the guests of honor of the King. The Queen was thoughtful enough to take Dakin aside and ask when it would be convenient for the royal dressmaker to call upon her mother, to measure all the ladies of Dakin's family for new dresses for the wedding, and the King's tailor would do the same for the men.

Dakin thanked the Queen politely and said she was sure any time would do, and that her mother would be delighted. She had no doubt about the truth of this, and could hardly imagine the excitement such news would bring to her sisters. For herself, Dakin could not work up the least enthusiasm for the wedding or anything connected with it, and drove home (in one of the royal carriages, the pony being brought back later) thinking all the way home how she could get out of going at all.

She and Gog had a long conversation on the way back. Gog asked a lot of questions about what had happened when the Evil One died, especially to his brothers who had been gargoyles.

"I can't understand why your spell didn't break at the

143

same time," said Dakin, who was expecting the tear magic to wear off at any moment.

"Oh, that's clear enough," said Gog. "The spell the Evil One put on me, just as I got to the edge of the wood seventeen years ago, couldn't be broken while I was beyond the foot of the mountain."

"Ah, I see!" said Dakin. "Then that means that if I take you back onto the mountain slopes again, the spell will be broken?"

"I should think so," said Gog. "If not . . . Well, you'll have to cry on me once a day. It would be better than nothing. After all, I did steal the ring. I deserve to be punished."

But Dakin lost no time at all, as soon as the carriage had set them down at their own door, in running off through the village as fast as she could in the direction of the farthest-away mountain.

27
BACK TO THE MOUNTAIN

IT WAS STRANGE TO cross the river again and be running toward that dark wall of trees, knowing now all that lay ahead. She entered the wood joyfully, and at once took Gog, who was now stiff and "dead" again, the tear magic having worn off, and set him down on the pine needles.

Nothing happened.

She picked him up and ran farther into the forest, holding him ahead of her, expecting every moment that he would change into a real, live troll like the others. But he didn't. On and on she ran. Why wasn't it working? The way was all uphill now, for she was well and truly on the slopes of the mountain. She began to get tired, for she was not yet perfectly strong after her adventures, but she kept going, watching the pine needles. The sun was going down. On she tramped, up and forward, hour after hour. . . . At last it grew dark. The moon rose. She was not afraid, though she felt cold and hungry.

"Don't worry, Gog," she said. "I think I know what we have to do."

The trees, at long last, began to thin, and the moonlight became brighter. She passed silently out between the last trunks, into the moonlit meadow.

It was even more beautiful than by day, if possible, and of course far more mysterious. Ahead the noble mountain crest rose straight before her, the moon silvering its snow; the black summit which had once been the ogre's castle now looked like the turrets and steeple of a great cathedral. Straight before her lay the meadow, bathed in the strange light, its long grasses whispering in the night breeze. And the cabin—

Dakin peered ahead. Where was it? This moonlight was strange! Everything seemed clear to her eyes, yet somehow she couldn't pick out the cabin. She began to run.

The cabin was gone. But it couldn't be! She ran on, her eyes straining to find it. She clutched Gog in her hand, running, running through the whispering silvery grasses. . . . Then—

Splash! She fell into deep water.

She gave a gasp and her mouth filled. She felt the cold water closing over her head. She kicked hard to make herself come up, but she kept sinking. In her hand Gog seemed to give a sudden twist, and then he was gone. Half drowning as she was, a new panic seized her and she groped wildly in the water. What if he sank to the middle of the world!

She could hold her breath no longer. Was this the end of her? Surely the saving waters of the Lithy Pool would not harm her!

But something had hold of her and was pulling her up. Her face burst clear, and all the water seemed to break into fragments of light around her. She drew a deep, deep breath, shook her head, and rubbed her eyes clear with both hands.

She looked. The first thing she saw was a young man.

He was standing on a smooth, grassy place. The moonlight was shining on him. He was watching her with dark, serious eyes. He was all that a young man should be—all that Prince Rally wasn't.

"Who are you?" asked Dakin with a gasp.

"Don't you know? I'm Ravik, the idiot."

For a moment they stared at each other.

"You're Croak," she whispered at last.

He shook his head. "Not anymore. Ravik. The idiot."

"Ravik—the scholar—gentle, kind, and generous."

"But a fool."

"You've paid for that. Eating flies for two hundred years . . ."

He did not smile. "Others have paid, too. I can't forgive myself."

"That's silly. It's all over."

147

"Yes," said Gog's voice, "it's all over."

He was standing beside them, a proper, full-grown troll, grinning from ear to ear.

"The Lithy water did it!" he said gleefully, capering

about. "Where are my brothers? I must say hello to them. Do you think they're still angry with me? Where can I find them?"

"They're living in Drackamag's cave," said Ravik. "Straight up there. An hour's walk should do it."

"When will I see you again, Gog?" asked Dakin.

"On your wedding day!" Gog called back over his shoulder. "We'll all come! I'll give your love to the others, and an invitation!" And he ran off, every few steps giving a little dancing jump into the air and clicking his heels together.

Ravik and Dakin turned to each other again. They were both still dripping wet.

"What did he mean, my wedding day?" asked Dakin.

"I don't know. I would love you to marry me, but I understand you swore you would marry only a prince. I'm not a prince."

Dakin blushed furiously and hung her head.

"I was the idiot when I said that," she said. "I wish I hadn't. Could I unswear, do you think?"

"We all make mistakes," said Ravik. "If you can forgive me for mine, I can easily forgive you for yours."

"Then I will marry you. Could it be, say, a week-today? Then I wouldn't have to go to the royal wedding."

Ravik looked rather stern. "The King would be disappointed. And don't you want your family to come to our wedding?"

"Yes, of course! And the brothers. And—"

"And who?"

"No, it's silly."

"Tell me."

"Well . . . the Voice. But how can a voice come to a wedding?"

Ravik put back his head and roared with laughter, but not unkindly. "Dakin," he said, "if the wedding is to be here, on the mountain, then the Voice will certainly be at it. For the Voice is the Voice of the mountain, the soul of the mountain, which has wakened at last from its long sleep. You woke it yourself, by the strength of your wish to come here; and by your goodness and courage when you did come, you made it powerful enough to help you defeat the Evil One that I, in my folly, brought here long ago." He put his hands on her shoulders. "Listen. Go to the Prince's wedding, collect your reward, and give it away to your family or the poor people of the village. Then, when it's over, you can come to me here and we'll be married. Only this time, remember that the cabin's been taken down! Otherwise you might fall into the pool again and spoil your new dress."

"Why did you take it down?" asked Dakin.

"It was my prison for two hundred years," said Ravik. "As soon as I'd been all over the mountain to make sure all the evil on it had been done away with, the first thing I did was to pull it down. But don't worry," he added, seeing her face, "I can build it up again. But bigger. Big enough for the two of us."

He kissed her soundly, and then Dakin said, "Do you

think, now the mountain's awake again, that it will begin to call people, as it did before—good people? It would be nice if we could start a village up here."

"It might happen. Not too soon, I hope. We have plenty of work to do here first."

"We shall be the prince and princess of the mountain," said Dakin.

"I must take you home. Your family shouldn't have to worry about you anymore."

The prince of the farthest-away mountain took her hand and they walked down through the moonlight glades of the wood together.